CORALIE

CHARLOTTE M. BRAEME

Coralie

Charlotte M. Braeme

© 1st World Library – Literary Society, 2005
PO Box 2211
Fairfield, IA 52556
www.1stworldlibrary.org
First Edition

LCCN: 2004195595

Softcover ISBN: 1-4218-0416-6
Hardcover ISBN: 1-4218-0316-X
eBook ISBN: 1-4218-0516-2

Purchase *"Coralie"*
as a traditional bound book at:
www.1stWorldLibrary.org/purchase.asp?ISBN=1-4218-0416-6

1st World Library Literary Society is a nonprofit
organization dedicated to promoting literacy by:

- Creating a free internet library accessible from any
  computer worldwide.
- Hosting writing competitions and offering book
  publishing scholarships.

CHAPTER I.

"Eighty pounds a year!" My reader can imagine that this was no great fortune. I had little or nothing to spend in kid gloves or cigars; indeed, to speak plain, prosaic English, I went without a good dinner far oftener than I had one. Yet, withal, I was passing rich on eighty pounds a year.

My father, Captain Trevelyan, a brave and deserving officer, died when I was a child. My mother, a meek, fragile invalid, never recovered his loss, but died some years after him, leaving me alone in the world with my sister Clare.

When I was young I had great dreams of fame and glory. I was to be a brave soldier like my dear, dead father, or a great writer or a statesman. I dreamed of everything except falling into the common grooves of life - which was my fate in after years. My mother, believing in my dreams, contrived to send me to college - we both considered a college education the only preliminary to a golden future. How she managed it out of her slender means I cannot tell, but she kept me at college for three years. I was just trying to decide what profession to adopt, when a letter came summoning me suddenly home.

My mother was ill, not expected to live.

When I did reach home I found another source of trouble. My sister Clare, whom I had left a beautiful, blooming girl of eighteen, had been ill for the past year. The doctors declared it to be a spinal complaint, from which she was not likely to recover, although she might live for years.

She was unable to move, but lay always on a couch or sofa. The first glimpse of her altered face, so sweet, so sad and colorless, made my heart ache.

All the youth and bloom had died out of it.

My mother did not live many days; at her death her income ceased, and I found myself, at twenty, obliged to begin the world as best I could, the sole protector of my invalid sister. The first step was to sell our little home, a pretty cottage at Hempstead, then to take lodgings nearer the city; after that I set vigorously to work to look for a situation.

Ah, me, that weary task! I wonder if any of my readers ever went quite alone, friendless, almost helpless, into the great, modern Babylon, to look for a situation; if so, they will know how to pity me. I spent many pounds in advertisements; I haunted the agency offices; I answered every advertisement I read - it seemed all in vain.

My father's regiment was then in India, but I wrote to several of the officers, who had known and valued him. Then, as a last resource, I looked up the few friends my mother had.

If there is one thing more dreary than looking for a situation, it is what is commonly called "hunting up

Charlotte M. Braeme

one's friends." I found many, but some were old and indifferent, others too much engrossed in their own affairs to have any time to devote to mine. Some shook hands, wished me well, promised to do all they could to help me, and before I had passed from their sight forgot my existence.

I gave up my friends. Their help in the hour of need is a beautiful theory, but very seldom put into practice.

Just as I was growing dull and dispirited, a friend upon whom I had not called, and whose aid I had not solicited, wrote to me and offered me a situation as clerk in his office, with a salary of eighty pounds per annum, to be afterward increased. God send to every weary heart the comfort this news brought to mine. I ran to Clare with the letter in my hands.

"Eighty pounds a year, darling!" I cried; "there is a fortune."

We had neither of us ever had much to do with money; we were quite ignorant of its value, how far it would go, what it would purchase, etc. It seemed an inexhaustible sum. We had cheap, comfortable apartments in Holloway - a room for my sister and two smaller rooms for myself. When I think of her patience, her resignation, her unvarying sweetness, her constant cheerfulness, my heart does homage to the virtue and goodness of women.

One fine morning in September I went for the first time to work. The office of Lawson Brothers was in Lincoln's Inn. The elder brother seldom if ever appeared; the younger was always there. He gave me a very kindly welcome, said he hoped I should not find my work tiresome, showed me what I had to do, and, altogether, set me at my ease.

I sighed many times that morning to find of how little use was my college education to me now and I sighed to think how all my dreams, all my hopes and aspirations, had ended behind a clerk's desk, with eighty pounds per annum in lieu of the fortune of which I had dreamed.

After a few days I became used to the novelty and did my best to discharge my duties well.

Hundreds of young men in London lead lives similar to mine, with very little variety; the only way in which I differed from them was that I had my sister Clare to provide for. Alas! how soon I found out what a small sum eighty pounds a year was! When we had paid the rent of our three rooms, set aside a small sum for clothes and a small sum for food, there was nothing left. Clare, whose appetite was dainty and delicate, suffered greatly. I could not manage to provide even a bunch of grapes for her; the trifling coppers I spent in flowers, that cheered her as nothing else ever did, were sorely missed.

How I longed sometimes to take home a ripe peach, a bottle of wine, an amusing book! But every penny was rigorously needed; there was not one to spare. How I pitied her for the long hours she spent alone in those solitary lodgings! A bright inspiration came to me one day; I thought how glad I should be if I could get some work to do at night, if it were but possible to earn a few shillings. I advertised again, and after some time succeeded in getting copying to do, for which I was not overwell paid.

Charlotte M. Braeme

I earned a pound - positively a whole golden sovereign - and when it lay in my hand my joy was too great for words. What should I do with one sovereign and such a multiplicity of wants? Do not laugh at me, reader, when I tell you what I did do, after long and anxious debate with myself. I paid a quarter's subscription at Mudie's, so that my poor sister should have something to while away the dreary hours of the long day. With the few shillings left I bought her a bottle of wine and some oranges.

That is years ago, but tears rise in my eyes now when I remember her pretty joy, how gratefully she thanked me, how delicious she found the wine, how she made me taste it, how she opened the books one after another, and could hardly believe that every day she would have the same happiness - three books, three beautiful new books! Ah, well! As one grows older, such simple pleasures do not give the same great joy.

It was some time before I earned another. It was just as welcome to me, and there came to me a great wonder as to whether I should spend the whole of my life in this hard work with so small a recompense.

"Surely," I said to myself, "I shall rise in time; if I am diligent and attentive at the office, I must make my way."

But, alas! the steps were very small, and the clerks' salaries were only increased by five pounds a year at a time. It would be so long before I earned two hundred a year, and at the same rate I should be an old man before I reached three hundred.

One morning - it was the 1st of May - bright, warm,

sunny day, the London streets were more gay than usual, and as I walked along I wondered if ever again I should breathe the perfume of the lime and the lilac in the springtime. I saw a girl selling violets and daffodils, with crocuses and spring flowers. I am not ashamed to say that tears came into my eyes - flowers and sunshine and all things sweet seemed so far from me now.

I reached the office, and there, to my intense surprise, found a letter waiting for me.

"Here is a letter for you, Mr. Trevelyan," said the head clerk, carelessly.

He gave me a large blue official envelope. If he had but known what it contained!

Some minutes passed before I had time to open it; then I read as follows:

"To Sir Edgar Trevelyan:

"Sir: We beg to inform you that by the death of Sir Barnard Trevelyan, and his son, Mr. Miles Trevelyan, who both died of the epidemic in Florence, you, as next of kin, will succeed. We are not aware that the late Sir Barnard had any other relatives. Crown Anstey, the residence of the late baronet, is ready at any time for your reception. If you can favor us with a call today, we will explain to you the different ways in which the late baronet's large fortune is invested. We have managed the Crown Anstey property for some years, and hope to have the honor of continuing our business relations with you. We are, sir, your

Charlotte M. Braeme

obedient servants,

"Moreland & Paine."

The letter fell from my hands and I looked at it in blank astonishment too great for words.

Sir Barnard Trevelyan! Crown Anstey! Why, the last time I ever heard those names my mother sat talking to me about this proud, stately cousin of my father - cousin who had never noticed either him or us by word or by look. I was curious, and asked many questions about him. She told me he had married some great lady, the daughter of a duke, and that he had two sons - Miles, the eldest, and Cecil. I remembered having heard of Cecil's death, but never dreamed that it could affect me.

Moreland & Paine! I knew the firm very well; they had large offices in Lincoln's Inn, and bore a high reputation. Suddenly my heart stood still. Why, of course, it was a jest - a sorry jest of one of my fellow clerks. There they were, looking at me with eager, wondering eyes - of course it was a jest. My heart almost ceased to beat, and I caught my breath with something like a sob.

They should not laugh at me; they should not read what was passing in my mind.

I put the letter calmly and deliberately in my pocket and opened my ledger. I fancied they looked disappointed. Ah! it was but a jest; I would not think of it.

I worked hard until the dinner hour, and then asked permission to absent myself for a time. Dinner was not in my thoughts, but I went quickly as I could walk to the office of Moreland & Paine.

CHAPTER II.

Mr. Paine was not in. Mr. Moreland was in his office. I went up the stairs, trembling, fearful of being abused for stupidity in taking the least notice of such a letter.

Mr. Moreland looked up when the clerk announced my name - looked up, bowed and positively rose from his seat. I took the letter from my pocket.

"I received this this morning, but, believing it to be a jest played upon me, I have not mentioned it. I have called to ask you if you know anything of it."

He took the letter from me with a strange smile.

"I wrote it myself last evening," he said, and I looked at him bewildered.

Good heaven! it was all true. To this moment I do not know how I bore the shock. I remember falling into a chair, Mr. Moreland standing over me with a glass of something in his hand, which he forced me to drink.

"Your fortune has a strange effect upon you," he said, kindly.

"I cannot believe it!" I cried, clasping his hand. "I cannot realize it! I have been working so hard - so hard for one single sovereign - and now, you say, I am rich!"

"Now, most certainly," he replied, "you are Sir Edgar Trevelyan, master of Crown Anstey and a rent roll of ten thousand a year."

I am not ashamed to confess that when I heard that I bowed my head on my hands and cried like a child.

"You have borne bad fortune better than this," said Mr. Moreland; and then I remember telling him, in incoherent words, how poor we had been and how Clare was fading away for want of the nourishment and good support I was utterly unable to find for her.

After a time I became calmer and listened while he told me of the death of the stately Sir Barnard and his eldest son. They had gone away together on a trip to Italy. Miles Trevelyan was very fond of pictures, and his father had given him permission to buy what he pleased for the great picture gallery at Crown Anstey.

They went together to Florence, where a fearful epidemic was raging. They, all unconscious of it, remained there for one night, caught it, and in two days both lay dead.

I asked how old was Miles, this eldest and favorite son. He told me twenty-seven. I asked again, had he never been married. He answered no; that, of course, if he had been married and had children, I should not be the heir to Crown Anstey.

"There was some little unpleasantness between father and son over a love affair," said Mr. Moreland. "I do not know the particulars. Mr. Miles Trevelyan was very proud and reserved. He mentioned it to us, but we heard no more of it."

"What am I to do next?" I asked him, nervously.

"You ought to go down at once to Crown Anstey. The bodies of the two gentlemen will be brought home for interment. They died on the 18th; this is the 22d. We spent three days in trying to find out your address. They will be at Crown Anstey, I should say, to-morrow. You should be there to receive them and to officiate as head mourner. Mr. Paine and myself will both be there, as a matter of course."

"Then I must ask Mr. Lawson's permission," I said, doubtfully.

Mr. Moreland laughed.

"He will soon give you that. You will find the master of Crown Anstey a powerful personage."

"There is another thing," I said, with a crimson flush burning my face; "I have but five shillings and sixpence in all the world."

He laughed aloud at this.

"I can advance you whatever you like, then - five hundred pounds or more."

The very mention of such a sum positively frightened me. Mr. Moreland looked very much amused.

"It will be some time," he said, "before you grow

accustomed to ten thousand a year."

At that moment we were interrupted by the arrival of another client. I rose to take my leave, with a check for three hundred pounds in my hand.

"You will go down to Crown Anstey to-night?" said Mr. Moreland, as he shook hands with me. "We shall be there to-morrow morning. You will make what arrangements seem best to you over the funeral."

So I went away, the most bewildered man in London. As I re-entered the office I felt ashamed of my suspicions over my fellow-clerks. They were all busy, while I - oh, heaven! could it be true?

Mr. Lawson evidently thought I had been drinking when I went, white and stammering, confused and hesitating, into his room. He looked very sternly at me.

"What do you want, Mr. Trevelyan? I am very busy."

I took out the letter again and laid it before him.

"Will you read that, sir?" I asked, "It will make you understand more quickly than I can, I am so confused."

He read it, then held out his hand to me.

"I congratulate you," he said. "Your poor father, the last time I saw him, spoke to me of his rich cousin. He never expected this. Sir Barnard had two fine, strong, healthy sons of his own then."

"My father could not have expected it less than myself. I have hardly ever heard the name of Crown Anstey,

16   Charlotte M. Braeme

and did not know that it was entailed property. I shall have to ask you to let me go this afternoon, sir."

He was perfectly willing, I was only at the office an hour, yet the news seemed to have spread. I promised the clerks a dinner when I returned, then once more I stood in the street, alone.

My brain was dizzy, my thoughts in a whirl. I remember taking a cab and driving to a shop into which I had often looked with longing eyes. I bought wine, grapes, peaches, flowers, dainty jellies - everything that I thought most likely to please my sister - and then drove home. I had resolved that I would not tell my good fortune to Clare all at once, lest there should be some fatal mistake unforeseen by any one. She looked up astonished when I entered the room, my arms full of fruit and flowers.

"Oh, Edgar!" she cried, "you have ruined yourself. Why you must have spent your whole week's money!"

I forgot now what fiction I told here - something of a friend of my father, who had left me a little money, and that I was going away that same evening on business.

"Shall you be long?" she asked, with so sad a face I did not like to leave her.

"Two or three days at the outside," I told her. Then I took twenty golden sovereigns from my purse and laid them before her, begging her not to want for anything while I was away.

She looked almost alarmed at such a quantity

of money.

"Twenty pounds, Edgar!" she cried. "How rich we are!" And I thought to myself, "if she only knew!"

Then I went into my own room, and my first action was to thank God for this wonderful benefit. I thanked Him with streaming eyes and grateful heart, making a promise - which I have never broken - that I would act as steward of these great riches, and not forget the needy and the poor.

At five o'clock I started for Thornycroft, the nearest town to Crown Anstey. The journey was not a very long one, but I took no heed of time. Was it all a dream, or was I in reality going to take possession of a new and magnificent home?

I reached the station - it was a large one. Thornycroft seemed to be a thriving town. No one was there to meet me. I went to the nearest hotel and ordered a carriage to Crown Anstey.

I can recall even now my ecstasy of bewilderment at the splendid woods, the beautiful park, the pleasure gardens. How long was it since I had felt tears rush warm to my eyes at the scent of the violets? Here were lime trees and lindens, grand old oaks, splendid poplars, beech trees, cedars, magnolias with luscious blossom, hawthorn, white and pink larches budding, and all were mine - mine. Then from between the luxuriant foliage I saw the tall, gray towers of a stately mansion, and my whole heart went out to it as my future home.

The birds were singing, the sun shining; all nature was

Charlotte M. Braeme

so beautiful and bright that my very soul was enraptured.

Then I caught a glimpse of gold from the laburnums, of purple from the lilacs, of white from the sweet acacia trees.

The carriage drove up a long grove of chestnut trees, and then for the first time I saw Crown Anstey. The western sunbeams fell upon it. I thought of that line of Mrs. Hemans:

"Bathed in light like floating gold."

They showed so clearly the dainty, delicate tracing, the large, arched windows. The house itself was built in the old Elizabethan style. I found afterward that it was called Crown Anstey because it had belonged in former years to one of the queens of England. The Queen's Chamber was the largest and best room in it. Report said that a royal head had often lain there; that the queen to whom the house had belonged had spent many of her sorrowful and happy hours there. The Queen's Terrace run all along the western wing, and was shaded by whispering lime trees. Afterward I found many relics of this ancient time of royal possessions - antique, out-of-the-way things, with the crown and royal arms of England upon them. I was not a little proud of these historical treasures. A broad flight of steps led from the lawn to a broad porch. As I passed under it I figured to myself the gorgeous splendor of other days, when "knights and dames of high degree" had entered there.

An old butler, evidently an old family retainer, was the first person I saw. He bowed low when I told him that I was Sir Edgar Trevelyan, "the heir come to take possession."

I went through the magnificent house like a man in a dream. Could it be possible that all this magnificence, all this grandeur, was mine? Mine, these grand old rooms, with furniture and hangings that once served a queen; mine, these superb pictures and statues, these gems of art, this profusion of gold and silver plate? I laughed and cried in the same breath. I make no pretensions to being a strong-minded hero, and I was overcome.

Then, when I had some short time alone, the butler, whose name was Hewson, came back and told me the Red Room was ready for my use. He had selected it as being the most comfortable. Afterward I could, of course, take what rooms I liked.

I found myself in a large, spacious chamber, called the Red Room, from the prevailing tint of everything in it being crimson. The three large windows were hung with crimson velvet; the carpet was crimson. I opened one of the windows and looked over the glorious landscape, so full of sunshine, flowers and beauty, that my heart thrilled within me, and my soul did homage to the great Creator.

Charlotte M. Braeme

CHAPTER III.

Half an hour later I was summoned to the dining-room, where dinner was laid for me. God knows that I had never coveted wealth or thought much of luxury - I had been content with my lot.

What did I think when I saw that stately dining-room, with its brilliant lights, the gold and silver, the recherche dishes, the odorous wines and rare fruits? My first feeling was one of wonder that fortune should have so overpowered me; my second was a fervent wish that such pleasant times could fall to every one.

I had finished dinner and enjoyed, for the first time in my life, a really prime cigar, when Hewson came into the library, evidently wishing to see me.

"I thought I had better tell you. Sir Edgar, that Mademoiselle d'Aubergne is in the drawing-room."

I looked at him in astonishment.

"Who is Mademoiselle d'Aubergne?" I asked.

"Do you not know, Sir Edgar?" he said, in great surprise.

"I have never even heard the name," I replied.

"Mademoiselle is the daughter of the late Sir Barnard's cousin; she has been living here for the past five years. Sir Barnard, I believe, adopted her. I thought perhaps Messrs. Moreland & Paine might have mentioned her."

They had perhaps forgotten to do so, and I felt quite at a loss what to do. However, if there was a lady in the house, I was bound to be courteous; so I went to the drawing-room.

I attempt no description of that magnificent room, its treasures of art, its statues, pictures, flowers, its wonders of bric-a-brac. For the first minute my eyes were dazzled, and then I saw -

Well, I had read in the old poets' descriptions of sirens' wondrous language, wondrous words telling of beauty almost divine in its radiance - of golden hair that had caught the sunshine and held it captive - of eyes like lode-stars, in whose depths men lost themselves - of lovely scarlet lips that could smile and threaten. I saw such loveliness before me now.

From the luxurious depths of a crimson velvet fauteuil rose a lovely woman, who advanced to meet me with outstretched hands. Her mourning dress fell in graceful folds around her tall, queenly figure, and from the same dark dress her fair face and golden head shone out bright and luminous as a jewel from a dark background.

"Sir Edgar Trevelyan," she said, "allow me to welcome you home."

Her voice was sweet and rich; she had a pretty, piquant accent, and the play of her lips as she spoke was

Charlotte M. Braeme

simply perfection.

"It is very lonely for you," she said. "There is great gloom over the house, it is all sad and dark; but the brightness will come back in time."

I touched the white hand she held out to me; it was warm and soft; the touch of those slender fingers had a magical effect.

"I must apologize for not having seen you before," I said, "but until five minutes ago I did not know you were in the house."

"No," she replied, with a faint sigh, "I can believe that."

"You must know," I continued, "that I am a complete stranger to the family. I never saw any of them in my life. I never heard the name more than five or six times."

"Then, as a matter of course," she said, "you never heard of me."

"I am at a loss to know whether I should address you as kinswoman or not," was my confused reply.

"It would take a bench of lawyers to decide," she said. "My mother was a favorite cousin of Sir Barnard. I think, but I am not sure, that once upon a time he was fond of her himself. My mother married a French gentleman, Monsieur d'Aubergne, and at her death Sir Barnard kindly offered me a home here, since I had no other."

"Is your father living?" I asked.

"Alas! no; he died when I was a child. There had been some quarrel between my mother and Sir Barnard; perhaps he never forgave her for marrying a Frenchman. During her lifetime he never wrote to her or took the least notice of me."

"And then offered you his home?"

"Then he adopted me," she said, looking earnestly at me; "treated me in every way as his own child. I have been with him ever since. I have no home except here at Crown Anstey, and I had not a sou in the world except what he gave me. Ah! I miss him so sorely."

A cloud came over her beautiful face, and her lips quivered. I sat down in sore perplexity with my inheritance. I had not certainly expected this. What was I to say to her - this beautiful and radiant woman, who seemed thrown upon my hands like a child? There was silence between us for some time, then she said, suddenly:

"How sad this is about poor Sir Barnard and his son, is it not? I thought at first that I should never recover from the shock. Miles was a very handsome man; so clever and full of spirits. I am told," she continued, "that the bodies are to be brought home to-night. Is it true, Sir Edgar?"

"I believe so. I am here to receive them and to preside at the funeral."

Her face grew a shade paler.

"I am so frightened and nervous at everything connected with death," she said.

"Your best plan will be to remain in your own room until it is all over," I suggested, and she seemed very grateful for the thought.

"Will you take some tea?" she asked, suddenly. "I always made tea for Sir Barnard and Miles."

Then she drew back shrinkingly, her face crimson.

"I beg your pardon," she said. "I forgot; I have no right to take the same place now."

What could I do but hasten to implore her not to yield to such an idea, to consider Crown Anstey her home, as it had been - at least for a time?

"You make me so happy!" she said; "but how can I - how can I stay here? I find it awkward to explain myself - how can I remain here with you?"

I hastened eagerly to explain that I had a sister, an invalid sister, and that I should be delighted if she would take an interest in her; and it pleased me to think how happy Clare would be.

"Then you wish me to remain here as a companion to your sister?" she said, slowly; and there was evidently some little disappointment in her face.

"Unless we can think of something more pleasant for you," I replied. "We can make that a temporary arrangement. In any case, permit me to say that I shall take the care of your future on my hands, as Sir

Barnard would have done."

"You are very kind," she said, thoughtfully; "I had no right to expect that. I did not anticipate anything of the sort."

We talked then, in low tones, about the late baronet and his son. Of Miles she said very little. Of Sir Barnard she told me many anecdotes, illustrating his pride, his grave, stately character, his intense love of caste, his conservatism. I felt almost as though I had known him before she had finished.

"And Miles," I said, "the poor young heir; how did you like him?"

Was it my fancy, the light flickering on her face, or did a quick shudder pass over it?

"Every one liked him," she said, slowly. "He was proud and reserved; yet he was a general favorite."

She was strangely quiet after that, and I suddenly remembered the drawing-room was hers. I rose, bidding her good-night.

"You shall be sure to hear the stir of the arrival, mademoiselle," I said; "do not let it disturb you. I should advise you to keep your room tomorrow until the funeral is over."

Yet, although I so advised her, it struck me that she did not feel any great amount of sorrow. I cannot tell why I had that impression, but it was very strong upon me.

Nine o'clock, and the arrival had not yet taken place.

Charlotte M. Braeme

The fragrant gloaming was giving way to night; there was promise of a bright moon, and the golden stars were peeping one by one. The night-wind was laden with odors, a thousand flowers seemed to have given their sweet breath to fan it. It would have been profanation to have lighted a cigar, so I went out on the Queen's Terrace and walked under the whispering lime trees, thinking of all that had passed in those few days.

Slowly but surely the conviction gained upon me that I did not like Coralie d'Aubergne. I ought, according to all authentic romances, to have fallen in love with her on the spot, but I was far from doing so. "Why?" I asked myself. She was very brilliant - very lovely; I had seen no one like her, yet the vague suspicion grew and grew. It was not the face of a woman who could be trusted; there was something insincere beneath its beauty. I should have liked her better if she had shown more sorrow for the awful event that had happened; as, it was, I could not help thinking that her chief emotion had been a kind of half fear as to what would become of herself.

Then I reproached myself for thinking so unkindly of her, and resolved that I would not judge her; after that I forgot mademoiselle. I heard the sound of carriage wheels in the distance, and, looking down the long vista of trees, I saw a hearse slowly driven up, and then I knew that the dead Trevelyans had been brought home.

The desolation and sadness of that scene I shall never forget - the hearse, the dark, waving plumes, the sight of the two heavy laden coffins, the servants all in mourning.

A room next the great entrance hall had been prepared; it was all hungwith black and lighted with wax tapers. In the midst stood the two coffins covered with a black velvet pall.

On the coffin of Miles Trevelyan, the son and heir, I saw a wreath of flowers. I asked several times who had brought it, but no one seemed to know.

I do not think that any one at Crown Anstey went to rest that night, unless it were mademoiselle. There was something in the event to move the hardest heart.

Father and son had left Crown Anstey so short a time since, full of health, vigor, strength and plans for the future. They lay there now, side by side, silent and dead; no more plans or hopes, wishes or fears. The saddest day I ever remember was the one on which I helped to lay my two unknown kinsmen in the family vault of the Trevelyans.

Charlotte M. Braeme

CHAPTER IV.

It was all over. The morning, with its sad office, had passed; the servants had gone back to their work; the blinds were drawn up, and light once more found its way into the darkened house. The will was read in the library; the whole of the property, entailed and unentailed, was left to his only son, Miles, and after him to his heirs. There was several legacies to his servants, but no mention was made of mademoiselle. I thought it strange at the time, afterward I understood it.

Of course, as the poor young Miles was dead without heirs, I, as next of kin, took his place. I faithfully carried out every wish expressed in the will. That same evening I sent orders to London for a splendid memorial window to be placed in the church, and while I sat wondering whether I had remembered everything that required attention, there came a rap at the library door. Mademoiselle would be glad if I could see her for five minutes.

I went at once to the drawing-room, knowing she would be there. She was dressed in the deepest mourning, and her face was very pale.

"I knew you would spare me a short time," she said. "I want to ask you a question that I could not ask any one else. Of course you were present when the will was read to-day?"

She raised her eyes to mine. I knew not what magnetism, what spell lay in them; but no other eyes were like them. They compelled attention; a man could no more release himself from their glance than he could fly. I was not at all in love with her, yet those eyes held me spell-bound.

"I want you to tell me," she said, "if there was any other will. Did - did Miles leave one?"

As she put the question to me I saw that her lips were parched and burning, her white fingers so tightly clenched that they left great red marks.

"No," I replied; "there was only one will, and that was Sir Barnard's."

A great calm fell over her. After some minutes she looked at me again.

"Was there any mention in that will of me?"

I told her none. Once more she raised those resistless eyes to mine.

"Then I am, indeed, alone in the world - alone and forsaken."

"Nay, nay!" I cried, eagerly; "do not say so. Clare will take care of you."

"And you?" she asked, in a voice that must have melted an anchorite.

"I will help her - or, rather, I will take care of you both."

"What is your sister like?" she asked, eagerly. "Is she very clever - very beautiful? Shall I be frightened at her?"

"She is the sweetest and most gentle of girls - doubly gentle from her great affliction."

"What affliction?" she asked eagerly, "you did not tell me there was anything the matter with her."

"She has a spinal complaint," I replied, "and is unable to move."

"Is it quite incurable?" she asked again.

"We hope not; perhaps a change of air may do something for her; but even at the best, it will be years before she is able to go about."

"I am so sorry," she said; "so very sorry. How sad for you and for her. I can understand why you want a companion for her; she can take no active share in the management of a large establishment like this."

"No, no share at all. We will not decide anything until my sister comes; but it seems to me that she will be most thankful to have you here, that you will be more useful to her than I can say. She would not be able to see guests, give orders or anything of that kind."

There was a strange light in her eyes, a strange, suppressed glitter in her face.

"When will your sister come?" she next inquired.

"I am going to-morrow to fetch her. There will be no need for you to make any alterations. You spoke of going away; there will be no need of that. I leave here to-morrow, and when my sister comes I suppose the sternest British propriety will be satisfied."

She smiled.

"I suppose so, too. And Sir Barnard has not even left me a mourning-ring? Well, I have so much less to be grateful for. The old servants were all remembered, I hope?"

"All of them. I will say good-night, mademoiselle; I have much to attend to. I shall hope to find you well when I return."

What a strange fascination her beauty had! I remember it with a shudder. Her face haunted me all night; I could not forget it.

The following morning I returned to London. I had yet to break the news of our fortune to Clare, and make arrangements for our journey to Crown Anstey.

People who wish to be philosophers tell you money is nothing. Certainly, as far as the spiritual and higher, holier interests of life go, it is not; but as far as this world is concerned, it is almost everything. I had been poor and friendless in London, and then it had seemed to me a desert; now I had money, it was another place - bright, cheerful, every one kind and friendly. I seemed to float in sunshine; the very air around me was elastic, full of hope; every step was a pleasure. What made the

Charlotte M. Braeme

difference? I was poor, and now I had money.

Clare was pleased to see me; she cried out in astonishment at my black clothes, so new and glossy.

"Edgar," she said, "I cannot understand you. You have money, clothes. How is it? What has happened?"

I knelt down by her side and took her in my arms.

"Clare," I said, "God has been very kind to us. All of our poverty and privations are ended. Will you be calm and brave if I tell you what it is?"

"They have taken you into partnership!" she cried, rapturously. "They have found out how clever and good you are!"

In the midst of my agitation I laughed at this very unbusiness-like idea.

"It is better than that, Clare. There need be no more business, no more work for me. You remember hearing my mother speak of my father's cousin, Sir Barnard Trevelyan, of Crown Anstey?"

"Yes, I remember it," she said. "I had almost forgotten."

"He is dead, and, sad to say, both his sons are dead. One died with him, and one died years ago. Now do you understand?"

"No," she replied. "They cannot have left us anything, because they did not know us."

"Sir Barnard and his only son died together, and the heir to Crown Anstey, the title and the whole of that vast fortune is - myself."

"You are not jesting, Edgar?"

"No; I am telling you the simple, perfect truth." And then, when she had recovered from what to her was really a shock, I gave her the whole history.

"I hope you will like Mademoiselle, Clare. She is so utterly friendless and alone that, unless we keep her with us, I do not know what is to become of her."

"I shall be sure to like her," she said. "My heart is so full of happiness that I shall love every one. O, Edgar, if I could but get well!"

Yes, that was the one drawback to our happiness. The bright, sweet sister, who would have enjoyed our prosperity so much, was a helpless invalid.

That same afternoon I went to the office and invited all my fellow clerks to a sumptuous dinner at a far-famed restaurant. I made some sad hearts light and happy with my money, thank God! Poor Stephen Knowsley had a sick mother and was three quarters behind with his rent. I gave him fifty pounds, and the tears that stood in his eyes were the sweetest thanks man could have. What gives such pleasure as plenty of money to help one's friends?

A comfortable invalid carriage was provided for Clare, and the journey did not fatigue her. We said good-by to the old life, the old privations, the old trials, and embarked on a new, smiling and sunny sea.

Another week saw us comfortably settled at Crown Anstey. The first bewilderment of our new position passed away, I began to feel more at my ease as master of that magnificent mansion, and on my sister's calm face I saw already signs of returning health.

We had a grand reception when I returned with Clare to Crown Anstey. The Anstey church bells pealed out merrily; the servants were all assembled; mademoiselle, fresh and beautiful as a morning star, was in the hall.

I saw the kindly looks of commiseration that followed my sister. All the servants in the house vied with one another who should he the most attentive. Coralie looked at me, with sweet, sisterly anxiety shining in her eyes.

The following day Coralie suggested we find two nice, large, lofty cheerful rooms for my sister's use. We decided upon two in the western wing - they both looked on the Queen's Terrace - large, lofty rooms, with the sun shining on them all day, each one containing two large windows, from which could be seen a glorious vista of trees and flowers.

Without saying one word to Clare, they were prepared for her. Books, music, pictures, statues, flowers, were all arranged in order; everything bright and beautiful was brought there. A small part of the room was partitioned off and made into a conservatory, where she could see the flowers bloom and hear the birds sing all the day long.

I have seen many lovely places since then, but none that looked to me so bright and beautiful as my sister's rooms. All that money could do to alleviate her sufferings was done. I ordered the easiest reclining chair, on which she could be gently moved from room to room, resolving in my own mind, no matter what went on in other parts of the house, that in her rooms there should be always sunshine and happiness.

Her joy when she was carried into them was most pretty and pathetic to see. Then, when she was fairly installed, I wrote to London for the celebrated Dr. Finlaison, and I placed her under his care. He gave me some little hope.

In the course of time, he said, with the best of attention, the most tender care and cheerful society, she would, he believed, recover so as to be once more able to take her place in the world; and the hour in which I heard that was, I do not hesitate to say, one of the very happiest of my life.

This part of my story has been, perhaps, commonplace. There was coming for me a different phase. If my reader thinks it too romantic, I can only say - it is true.

Charlotte M. Braeme

CHAPTER V.

It was some little time before I asked Clare how she liked Coralie, then the answer was most diplomatic.

"I am so very sorry for her, Edgar, and so pleased that she has a home with us."

She never said more than that, or less. Knowing her amiable character, I came to the conclusion that she did not like her, but was too good-natured and kind-hearted to say so.

Mademoiselle, as she was called in the household, was very kind to my sister. She engaged a maid, whose only business was to wait upon her; and more than that, she spent some hours, at least, every day in her room. She attended to her flowers, fed her birds, selected her books, played and sang to her, read to her, talked to her in her bright, lively way, superintended her dress, so that I always saw my darling exquisitely attired; and yet I could not see that Clare liked her.

She soon made herself almost indispensable. She gave orders to the housekeeper and cook, she managed everything; she received our visitors and entertained them with marvelous grace and courtesy; she understood all the affairs of the estate; in fact, she was, to all intents and purposes, mistress of the house.

I insisted upon making her a very handsome allowance, which, after a little resistance, she accepted.

For a time everything went on most prosperously. How I loved my new life no words of mine can tell. The luxury of having plenty of money, of being able to do what I liked with my time, of seeing my sister so happy, of being altogether without those dark fears for the future which so often beset those whose lot is hard work and very limited means - I thanked God for it all.

I had made the acquaintance of most of the tenants on the estate, and my neighbors had begun to call upon me. It was surprising how every one liked, or, I may say, loved, my sister Clare. That invalid couch of hers became a kind of center of society.

One morning I saw some cards lying on the hall table. Coralie was standing near when I took them up. "Sir John Thesiger," "Lady Thesiger."

"That is a new name," I said to mademoiselle.

When she took the card from my hand and saw it, a dark look came over her face; I saw her lips close more firmly.

"Have you not heard of the Thesigers? I thought every one knew Sir John. They live at Harden Manor, about five miles from here."

"Are they old friends of the family?" I asked.

Again the darkening look and the tightening lips.

"Both Sir Barnard and Miles knew them, but I cannot

Charlotte M. Braeme

say whether they were very great friends. Shall you call?"

She asked the question carelessly, but I saw that she was awaiting my reply with painful anxiety.

"Yes, I shall go; I like to be on friendly and intimate terms with all my neighbors. Sir John is the Tory member for Chingwell, is he not?"

"Yes," she replied, shortly.

"And next year I hope to be returned for Anstey, so that, of all men, I shall probably find him the most useful of acquaintances."

She turned away, and a sudden conviction came over me that, for some reason or other, Coralie d'Aubergne did not like the Thesigers. I rode over to Harden Manor on the day following, and found Sir John at home.

I liked him at first sight - a frank, kind-hearted English gentleman. He was pleased to see me, and we spent some time talking over the late baronet and his son. He told me something I had not heard from Coralie - that there had been some slight misunderstanding between father and son. He asked me if I would join the ladies, who were in the drawing-room. I was only too pleased.

"Lady Thesiger was Sir Barnard's confidant. He consulted her about everything - indeed, we were such near and dear friends that you must forgive me if I cannot look upon you as a stranger."

Entering a very pretty drawing-room, long low and old-fashioned, I saw two ladies, one a matron, the other a lovely young girl. Sir John introduced me to his wife and then to Agatha, his daughter.

Looking up, I saw my fate. Never believe those cold-natured, cold-hearted people who tell you that love grows from respect. It does not. It comes into existence all at once - suddenly, as a flower is kissed into color by the sun. When I entered Harden Manor, I was heart-whole, fancy-free, loving no one but Clare; after one upward look in Agatha Thesiger's face, I loved her with a love that was my doom.

Sir John looked at me in amazement.

"I - I did not know you had a daughter, Sir John."

"Ah! but I have, and a very precious one, too. Poor Sir Barnard was very fond of Agatha; he used to call her his sunbeam. I was almost jealous of him at times."

"There was no need, papa," said a sweet voice, the very sound of which made me tremble.

Why had mademoiselle never mentioned this young girl, so fair, so lovely? Why had she told me nothing about her? I should like to describe her, reader, so as to make you love her. She was tall, very little above the medium height, slender, graceful, with a delicate, arched neck and the "fairest face the sun e'er shone on." Not beautiful - that word would not describe her; fair, sweet and lovely. She had no brilliant or vivid coloring; her complexion was clear, with the faintest rose-bloom; her eyes large and blue, her lips sweet and sensitive; a white brow and a wealth of soft, brown hair. She was no queenly beauty; she had not Coralie's brilliancy and bright coloring, but she was the fairest

Charlotte M. Braeme

and most lovable girl who ever made a man's heart glad.

I did not know how the next few minutes passed. Sir John and Lady Thesiger were talking about the neighborhood, and I was thinking that if Agatha bid me lie down there at her feet and die for her sweet sake, I should do so with a smile.

When I came to my senses, Lady Thesiger was asking me if I would dine with them the week following; they were expecting some visitors from London. I am sure she must have thought me almost an imbecile, I answered her in such a confused, hesitating way.

All the time Agatha sat opposite to me, her lovely eyes drooping over the drawing on which she was engaged when I entered. I could bear it no longer; come what might, I must see those eyes. I went over and stood by her side.

Alas! I had rarely, if ever, spoken to any young ladies except Clare and Coralie. I had crossed the room purposely to speak to her. Standing by her chair, every word I had ever known in my life died from memory, I could not think of one thing to say.

Bending over the picture, I asked if she were fond of drawing, and then I hated myself for the utter imbecility of the question.

When at once the blue eyes were raised to mine all constraint died away; they kindled a fire in my heart that nothing could ever extinguish.

"Miss Thesiger," I said, "I should be so pleased if I

could excite your interest in my sister."

"Have you a sister?" asked Lady Thesiger. "I did not know it; I am afraid she will think me very remiss."

I told them all about Clare, speaking, as was my fashion, with my heart upon my lips, telling them of her sweetness, her patience, her long illness, her cheerful resignation. Agatha forgot her reserve, Lady Thesiger looked deeply interested, and when I had finished speaking, the tears were in my eyes.

Lady Thesiger held out her hand.

"You have quite touched my heart, Sir Edgar; I shall not rest until I have seen Miss Trevelyan."

"Nor I," added the daughter.

I turned eagerly to her.

"You will come over to see my sister? I should be so grateful; she would welcome you so warmly. I have always longed for her to have a friend."

There was a slight constraint in the faces of mother and daughter. I wondered what it meant. Lady Thesiger was the first to speak.

"We shall be delighted to do all that lies in our power to soften Miss Trevelyan's terrible affliction. Pray, pardon me, Sir Edgar, but is Mademoiselle d'Aubergne still at Crown Anstey?"

"She is staying there as a companion to my sister, who is utterly incapable of taking any share in the

Charlotte M. Braeme

management of the house."

"You must find a wife," said Sir John. "I should say myself that Crown Anstey requires a mistress."

I longed to say there and then how I should pray him to give me his daughter for a wife. Our eyes met. She must have read my thoughts, for her face grew crimson, nor did I catch another glimpse of those lovely eyes during my visit.

It was with difficulty I could tear myself away. Sir John, who was a great connoisseur in horses, went with me to see Bonnie Prince. While we stood on the lawn he turned to me with a constrained smile.

"So mademoiselle is still at Crown Anstey?" he said. "I suppose she is as beautiful as ever?"

"Tastes differ," I replied, oddly. "Her beauty is not according to my idea."

His kindly face cleared.

"That is right; she is of the siren order; some people would find her irresistible. Now, pardon me if I say one word. I have known the lady for five years, and know nothing against her, still mistrust her without knowing why. You are young, new to the world; new, perhaps, to the influence of great womanly beauty; keep your heart safe. Do not let Mademoiselle d'Aubergne take it from you."

"There is no fear," I replied, with a light laugh. "Some day, Sir John, I will tell you where my heart has found its home."

"I am glad you know how to take a hint given in all kindness," he said, cordially. "As my old friend's heir and representative, my heart warms to you."

I left Harden Manor a changed man. The very earth around seemed changed to me; the sky wore a deeper blue; the grass a fairer green; there was new music in the birds' songs and in the whisper of the wind, new hope in my own heart, new beauty all around me. That was the beginning of the glamour posts call frenzy, men call love.

Mademoiselle was out on the lawn as I rode up to the door. She came to meet me, her glittering eyes on my face.

"Have you enjoyed your visit?" was the first question she asked.

"More than I ever enjoyed anything in my life. You did not tell me what a beautiful neighbor I had at Harden Manor."

"I never thought of it," she replied, carelessly. "Agatha Thesiger is only a school-girl."

"Then school-girls are very different from what I thought them," was my reply, and mademoiselle turned away with a strange smile.

CHAPTER VI.

No matter what I did, that face was always before me. If I read it looked up at me with sweet, serene eyes from the pages of my book. It rose between me and the blue heavens. I saw it in every flower. It haunted me until I could have cried out for respite from the pleasure that was yet half pain.

Poets sing of the joy and the rapture of love. Who knows its pain? For pain it surely is when no sleep comes near you, and the every-day duties of life only weary you, and your sole desire is to dream over looks and words you cannot forget. It is surely pain when a thousand doubts assail you, when you weigh yourself in the balance and find yourself wanting.

A hundred times each day I found myself wondering whether Sir John would think me good enough for his daughter. She was not his heiress, I knew, for he had a son at college, but she was lovely, high-born, accomplished, and my one great puzzle was whether he would think me a good match for her.

Other doubts came to madden me. Perhaps she was already engaged. She had doubtless a number of admirers. Who was I that I should dare to hope for her favor?

It was only two days since I had seen her, and I longed to see her again. A fierce, wild desire to look once more into that sweet face took possession of me. When my longing was gratified the very gates of Paradise seemed opened to me. One beautiful morning Lady Thesiger and Agatha came over to Crown Anstey. It so happened that I was in Clare's room when they arrived, and Coralie, too, was there, attending to the flowers, giving them fresh water, cutting off dead leaves and gathering the fairest buds.

Lady Thesiger and Miss Thesiger were suddenly announced. Clare looked eagerly, and I just caught the dark, bitter expression on Coralie's face; then they entered. As a matter of course, I introduced Lady Thesiger first. She stooped down to kiss the sweet face that seemed to win universal love. Then I remember taking Agatha's hand and leading her up to Clare. What could they have thought of me? I forgot everything except that the two women I loved best were there together.

Lady Thesiger then turned toward mademoiselle. There was no kindly hand extended, no warm greeting, no friendly words. Lady Thesiger made the most formal of bows, Coralie returned it by one more formal still, Agatha did the same, and a strange, constrained silence fell upon us all.

Without a word mademoiselle quitted the room. The beauty of her face was not pleasant in that moment; there was a glitter in her eye, a compression of her lips that might have told any one to beware. Lady Thesiger became her own natural self after Coralie's departure; she talked so kindly to Clare that I could have kissed her hand in gratitude.

I took Miss Thesiger to show her my sister's flowers; for no word of mine would those lovely eyes look up. She was not shy; her grace of manner was too perfect for that, but she was evidently afraid to look at me, and I reproached myself that I had perhaps frightened her at first.

Patiently I showed her flower after flower, perfect bud and perfect blossom, the little white doves I had tamed, the birds of bright plumage I had bought to amuse my sister. I showed her the little fountains that rippled all day, the rocks and ferns. She admired everything.

"Your sister must be happy in spite of her illness," she said to me.

But I could bear those drooping eyes no longer.

"Miss Thesiger," I said, hurriedly, "do not be unkind to me. I know I am very presumptuous, but do, pray do, give me one kind look before you go."

Then she raised her eyes and looked at me. Alas! my tell-tale face. They fell again, and the crimson flush mounted to her white brow. I could say no more to her after that. She went to her mother's side, and they talked to Clare until it was time for lunch.

I asked if they would remain and take lunch with my sister. They consented, and when it was arranged I sent to ask Coralie if she would join us. Her answer was that she was busily engaged and begged we would excuse her. Again I felt sure that Lady Thesiger looked considerably relieved.

Every moment I was falling more deeply and more

helplessly in love, and yet across all my rapturous thoughts of Agatha came doubt and wonder as to why they did not like Coralie.

Strange; she had the beauty of a siren, the grace and wit of a queen of society, the talents and accomplishments of a complete woman of the world, yet no one seemed to like her. How could it be?

Lady Thesiger rose at last, declaring that she was ashamed at the length of her visit. When they were gone I went back to Clare. She looked up at me with a smile; there was a bright flush of animation on her face.

"How much I like them, Edgar! How kind Lady Thesiger is, and Agatha! Oh, brother, how I wish I had a sister like her!"

I thought I would ask her to solve my doubt.

"Clare," I said, gravely, "I want you to explain something to me. You, being a woman, can understand women. Tell me how it is no one likes Coralie. She is beautiful and clever; why is it no one cares for her?"

My sister looked at me uneasily.

"I cannot tell. I wish you would not ask me, Edgar."

"Nay; tell me what you think?"

"Then I fancy it must be because she is not quite sincere. I do not like saying anything so unkind. You must not let it prejudice you against her; but she gives me always the impression of a person who leads two lives - one that everybody sees and one that nobody understands save herself."

"How old should you imagine her to be?" I asked; and again my sister looked uneasily at me.

"We have been in the habit of considering her a young girl," she replied, "but do you know, Edgar, I believe she is more than thirty?"

"It is impossible!" I cried. "Why, Clare, she does not look a day more than eighteen."

"She is what the French people call well preserved. She will look no older for the next ten years. She has a girl's figure and a girl's face, but a woman's heart, Edgar, I am sure of it."

"She is thirty, you say, and has been here for five years; that would make her a woman of twenty-five before she left France. A French woman of twenty-five has lived her life."

"That is just what I mean," she replied. "Rely upon it, for all her girlish face and girlish ways, Coralie d'Aubergne has lived hers."

"Clare," I asked, half shyly, "how do you like Miss Thesiger?"

A look bright as a sunbeam came over my sister's face.

"Ah! hers is a beautiful nature - sweet, frank, candid, transparent - no two lives there, Edgar. Her face is as pure as a lily, and her soul is the same. No need to turn from me, dear; I read your secret when she came in. If you give me such a sister as that I shall be grateful to you."

"Then you think there might be some chance for me if I asked her to become my wife?"

"Assuredly. Why not?"

She said no more, for at that moment Coralie returned; she had been in the garden gathering some flowers for Clare. The brightest bloom was on her face; the brightest light was in her eye. Looking at her, it was impossible to believe that she was anything but a light-hearted happy girl.

She glanced round the room.

"Your visitors are gone," she said. "I felt sure they were staying for dinner."

"Coralie," I asked, "Lady Thesiger tells me she has been here a good deal, yet you do not seem to be on very intimate terms with her?"

"No," she said, with that frank smile that was lovely enough to charm any one. "I neither like nor admire Lady Thesiger."

Clare uttered a little cry of astonishment.

"Why not?" I asked.

"I should not like to prejudice you against them, Sir Edgar; but as you ask me, I will tell you. The Thesigers have but one object."

"What is it?" I inquired for she had paused abruptly, and seemed to be entirely engrossed in her flowers.

"The one aim they have had in view for several years past is to see Agatha mistress of Crown Anstey. She was educated solely and entirely for that purpose."

"I do not believe it!" cried Clare, indignantly.

"I should never expect you to do so. You are too unworldly - too good; you know nothing of the manners of fashionable people. Sir Barnard knew it. They fairly hunted him down; they were always driving over here, or asking Sir Barnard and Miles there; they were continually contriving fresh means to throw Miles and Agatha together."

I would not please her by showing my anger.

"Perhaps," I said, carelessly, "Miles admired her; he may even have been her lover."

She turned to me with a strange, glittering smile, a look I could not fathom on her face.

"No," she replied: "Miles knew all about it; he was too sensible to be caught by the insipid charms of a mere school-girl. Sir Barnard was not so wise; he would have liked to join the two estates - he spoke of it very often - but Miles never gave the matter a serious thought."

There was such unconcealed bitterness in her words and look - such malice in that glittering smile, I turned away half in disgust.

"All our neighbors understand Lady Thesiger's politics," she continued; "they have been a source of great amusement for some time."

"Miss Thesiger is not a day above eighteen," I said, fairly angry at last; "so that there can not have been much time for manoeuvring."

"Ah!" she said, "how I admire you, Sir Edgar. That simple, noble faith you have in women is most beautiful to me; one sees it so seldom in those who have lived always among fashionable men and women."

A little speech that was intended to remind me how strange and fresh I was to this upper world. I began to find something like dislike to mademoiselle growing up in my mind; but I spoke to her of the Thesigers no more.

CHAPTER VII.

It seems an unmanly thing to write of a woman - my own face flushes hotly as I write the words - but to make my story plain the truth must be told. I could not help seeing that Coralie d'Aubergne was growing to like me very much.

To describe how a man woos a woman is a task pleasant enough. It is natural and beautiful; he is in his place then and she in hers; but who would not shrink from the hateful task of describing how a woman woos a man?

God bless all women, say I! My life has been a long one, and my experience of them bids me say they are almost all angels. I have found them true, tender and earnest. I could tell stories of women's quiet heroism that would move any one's heart. God bless them, one and all - they are the chief comfort in life!

Still even I, who love and respect them so much, am compelled to own that there are women wanting in purity and goodness, in modesty and reserve. I grieve to say Coralie d'Aubergne was one of them. She pursued me, and yet it was all so quietly done that she left me no room to speak - no ground on which to interfere.

If I went out in the gloaming to smoke a cigar, as I liked best to do among the sighs of the roses, in a few minutes that beautiful, fair face was sure to be smiling at my side. She had a pretty, picturesque way of throwing a black lace shawl over her shoulders and of draping it round her head, so making her face look a thousand times more fair.

She would come to me with that graceful, easy, dignified walk of hers and say:

"If I am not intruding, Sir Edgar, I should enjoy a few minutes with you."

She had a wonderful gift of conversation - piquant, sparkling and intellectual. If I had been the dullest of the dull, I should have known that such a woman would not pass her life as a companion unless she had some wonderful end in view. She was far too brilliant. She would have made a good ambassadress, for she could make herself all things to all men. No matter what subject interested you, on that she could speak. She seemed to understand every one intuitively; one's likes, dislikes, tastes. She had a wondrous power of reading character. She was worldly with the worldly, good with the good, romantic with the young, sensible with the old. To me she was always the same. Sometimes, when I saw her coming to meet me along those paths where the rose leaves lay dead, I felt inclined to go away and leave her; but natural politeness came to my aid. Then when she had talked to me for a few minutes, a strange, subtle charm would steal over me.

I knew her well-chosen compliments were all flattery. I knew she was pursuing me for some object of her own.

Charlotte M. Braeme

Yet that charm no words can describe was stronger than my reason. Away from her I disliked her; my judgment was all against her; in her presence no man could help being fascinated.

I thank Heaven that I had the shield of a pure and holy love; I was but a weak man, and nothing else saved me. If there came a wet day, or one that was not pleasant for walking, she had a thousand ways of making time fly. She played billiards as well as any man; she read aloud more beautifully and perfectly than I have ever heard any one else. She made every room she entered cheerful; she had a fund of anecdote that never seemed to be exhausted.

But the time she liked best for weaving her spells was after sunset, before the lamps were lighted.

"You are fond of music, Sir Edgar," she would say to me. "Come, and I will sing you some songs I used to sing years ago."

And she did sing. Listening to her, I could well believe in the far-famed Orpheus lute. It was enough to bewilder any man. She had a sweet, rich voice, a contralto of no ordinary merit, and the way in which she used it was something never to be forgotten.

There was a deep bay-window in the drawing-room, my favorite nook; from it there was a splendid view of waving trees and blooming flowers. She would place my chair there for me and then sing until she sung my senses away. There was such power, such pathos, such passion, in her voice that no one could listen to it unmoved.

Then, when she had sung until my very senses were steeped in the sweet madness of her music, she would come and sit, sometimes by my side, sometimes on a Turkish cushion at my feet.

And then - well, I do not like to say more, but as women can woo, she wooed me. Sometimes her hand, so warm and soft, would touch mine; sometimes, to see what I was reading, she would bend over me until her hair brushed my cheek and the perfume of the flowers she always wore reached me.

Thank God, I say again, that I was shielded by a pure love.

"How I love Crown Anstey!" she said to me one evening; "if I were asked to choose between being crowned Queen of Great Britain or mistress of Crown Anstey, I should prefer to remain here."

How well I remember that evening! The golden summer was dying then; the flowers seemed to be yielding all their sweetest perfumes to it; there was a lovely light from the evening sky that lingered on the tufted lime trees; the birds were singing a faint, sweet vesper hymn; the time so soon was coming when they were to cross the sunny seas in search of warmer climes.

I had been reading to Clare, but she did not seem to be quite so well and asked to be left alone.

"Let Coralie play and sing for you, Edgar," she said; "I shall hear the faint sound of it, and it will make me happy, because I shall know you are well amused." I did not like to tell her how distasteful Coralie's playing

Charlotte M. Braeme

and singing were to me. We went into the drawing-room together. I saw how everything was prepared for me; there were fresh flowers, my favorite periodicals, my favorite chair, placed in the nook I liked best.

"I shall sing to you some gay French chansons," said Coralie, "and we will leave the door open so that Clare may hear them."

A few moments later and I was in an atmosphere of delight. The rich, sweet music rose and fell; it cheered me like strong wine.

Then after a time its character changed; it was no longer gay, triumphant and mirthful. The very spirit of love and pathos seemed to breathe through it. My heart beat; every nerve thrilled; every sense answered to these sweet, soft words.

It ceased then, and Coralie came over to the bay-window. She sat down upon the Turkish curtains, and looked with longing eyes at the light on the trees and flowers. There was a softened expression on her face, a flush as of awakened emotion, a new and brighter light in those dark, dangerous eyes. The white fingers trembled, the white bosom heaved as though she had felt deeply the words she had been singing.

Then it was said she would rather be mistress of Crown Anstey than Queen of Great Britain.

I laughed, not knowing what to say.

"Crown Anstey ought to thank you very much," I said. "You pay it a great compliment."

"My heart is here," she continued, those dreamy eyes still fixed upon mine. "I think if any one were to say to me, 'You must l eave Crown Anstey,' I should die."

All the music on earth seemed embodied in those few words.

"I should die," she repeated, "just as a flower dies when it is torn from the soil it has taken deep root."

"Why do you speak of such things?" I asked. "No one thinks of your going; this is your home."

"In my happiest hours the fear lies heaviest upon me," she replied. "No one has ever spoken of my going, that is true; but I have common sense, and common sense tells me if certain events happen I must go."

"What events do you mean?" I asked, all unconsciously.

She sighed deeply.

"If you were to be married, Sir Edgar - Cousin Edgar, I like to say best - then I must go."

"I do not see the necessity."

"Ah! you do not understand; women are all jealous. I have grown so accustomed to perform a hundred little services for you, they make the pleasure and sunshine of my life. To be able to do some little thing to help you is the highest earthly joy that I can ever know. When you are married, Sir Edgar, your wife will take all this happiness from me."

"I do not see why," I replied, dryly, inwardly wishing myself safe in Clare's room.

"Ah! you do not understand - men never can understand the love of women. Wives, above all, are so very jealous. Fancy, if ever I wanted to make your tea, or get anything ready for you, she would be angry, and I should be wretched."

"In that case you must make tea for Clare instead of me."

"If I am anywhere near you, I must always attend to you before every one and anything in the wide world," she said, impulsively.

"You are making very sure that my wife will not like you," I said. "What if I have no wife?"

She shook her head gravely.

"You will marry, Sir Edgar. All the Trevelyans of Crown Anstey marry, as becomes the head of a grand old family. You will marry, and your wife will be the happiest woman in the world."

"I may be a modern Bluebeard, Coralie."

"No; you will not. Ah, me! To go away and leave Crown Anstey - to leave you - I shall feel like Eve driven forth from Paradise to die."

My hand lay carelessly on the back of a chair. She bent down swiftly and laid her burning lips upon it. I would not tell - my face flames as I write the word - but unless you know all, reader, you will not understand my story.

She laid her warm, soft lips upon it! And though I did not love her - did not even trust her - the magnetic touch thrilled every nerve. I took my hand away.

"Ah, cousin!" she said, looking at me with those dark, dangerous eyes, "you love even your dog Hector better than me."

She was so near to me that the perfume from her flowers reached me. It was by a desperate effort I broke the spell.

"This room is insufferably warm," I said; "I am going into the garden. You had better see if Clare wants anything, Coralie."

So, like many another man, I ran away, not knowing how to meet my fair adversary on equal grounds.

Charlotte M. Braeme

CHAPTER VIII.

Walking among the whispering leaves, the conclusion I came to was that I must take some precaution, or Coralie d'Aubergne would marry me whether I was willing or not. A siren is a faint shadow compared with a beautiful woman resolved to win a man whether he wants winning or not.

Why not risk my fate and ask Agatha to be my wife? There was a faint hope in my heart that she would not refuse me, yet she was so modest, so retiring, that though I had most perseveringly sought her favor since the first moment I had seen her, I could not tell whether she cared for me or not.

To judge by Coralie's standard, she did not like me. In all our conversation it half maddened me to see the lovely eyes I loved so dearly dropped shyly away from me.

It may not be a very elegant comparison, but she always reminded me of some shy, beautiful bird. She had a bright, half-startled way of looking at me. Several times, when I met her suddenly, I saw the lovely face flush and the little hands tremble.

Did she love me or did she not? I could not tell. Of whom should I take counsel? There was a bird singing over me; I wondered if that sweet night-song was all of love. Alas! that I had not been more into the world of women - their ways and fashions were all mysteries to me.

"Faint heart never won fair lady," says the old proverb, and it ran through my mind. I resolved to try my fortune. If she did not love me, why then, life held nothing more for me. If I could not win her I would never ask the love of woman more, but live out my life with Clare.

Like many other anxious lovers, I lay awake all night, wondering what I should say to her, how I should woo her, in what words I should ask her to be my wife. When day dawned I was still undecided, only that it was to be.

"You are going away early," said Coralie, as I ordered my horse. "Surely you will not be away all day, Sir Edgar?"

"I am going to Harden Manor, and cannot say when I shall return. Do not wait dinner for me - I may dine there."

"It will be a long, dark day," she said, with a sigh. "Do not be late - every hour will seem like two."

She hovered round me, asking many questions, evidently seeking to know my business there. When my horse was brought to the door, she came to me with a delicate spray of heliotrope.

"Let me fasten this in your coat, Sir Edgar. No gentleman looks completely dressed without a flower.

Charlotte M. Braeme

You do not know what heliotrope means. Men never - or, at least, very seldom - care for the sweetest of all languages - the language of flowers. What that heliotrope means, cousin, I say to you."

It was not until some weeks afterward that, looking quite accidentally over an old book, I discovered the spray of heliotrope meant, "I love you."

The beautiful picture of this fair, passionate woman died from my mind as I went to seek one a thousand times more fair. How well I remember the day - the golden sunshine, the fragrant wind, the blooming flowers, as I rode forth to win my love! It seemed to me that the summer skies smiled on me, and the singing birds wished me joy.

The way to Harden Manor lay through green, flowery lanes and a shady highroad. It seemed long because my heart sighed to be with her; yet short because I was so uncertain what to say, and how my wooing would end.

I reached the manor at last. Sir John was from home. Lady Thesiger and Agatha were busily engaged in making pretty fancy articles for a grand fancy fair that was to be held - for the benefit of some out-of-the-way people - by special permission of His Grace the Duke of Fairholme in the grounds of Fairholme Castle.

Lady Thesiger looked up when I entered, with a smile.

"Good morning, Sir Edgar; I am very glad to see you. Agatha and I were just wishing we had a gentleman to help us. Are you willing to assist us for a day?"

My face flushed hotly with delight.

"Am I willing to give myself a day of Utopian delight, Lady Thesiger? Most certainly. I will do anything - I can be very useful. I can mount drawings, frame photographs, sketch and design, and my humble talents are all yours."

Then Agatha looked at me, and the glance of those eyes was so sweet I almost lost myself.

"The Cherokee Indians, or whatever they are called, will be much obliged to you," she said. "I cannot call working for them 'Utopian delight;' my fingers ache with this stiff cardboard."

"You willfully misunderstand me, Miss Thesiger; the delight consists in being with you, not in working for the Cherokees. Save that I shudder when I hear that they have eaten a missionary, they have no particular interest for me."

Lady Thesiger smiled.

"You must work, not talk, Sir Edgar. Sit down here, pray, and if you think Miss Trevelyan will be uneasy, I will send a servant to tell her that you will remain here for lunch and for dinner."

"I prepared her for that emergency; now give me something to do for the Cherokees."

My hands were soon filled. It was pleasant sitting there in that fragrant, sunny drawing-room, with two of the most gracious and graceful women in England. Yet it was hard. I had gone there purposely to tell the story of my love, and now I was condemned to sit for hours by Agatha's side and say nothing to her.

Charlotte M. Braeme

"Perhaps fortune may favor me," I thought; "Lady Thesiger may leave the room, and then I will not lose a moment."

How fervently I blessed these Cherokees before the day was ended no one will ever know. Lady Thesiger never left us; Agatha worked very hard. Looking at the sweet, calm, high-bred face, I wondered if she knew that a lover, with his heart on fire, sat near her.

Lunch came - we went to the dining-room. Lady Thesiger told us we had only half an hour to spare; she had promised the duchess to send everything in that evening, and she did not wish to break her word.

"It is worse than slavery," I said, and Lady Thesiger laughed, little knowing why I was so impatient.

Back again to work. Happily, all was finished, and the servants were called in to pack the pretty, fragile articles.

"Now I shall have five minutes," I thought to myself, "and I will find out whether she cares for me or not."

Alas! there was the dressing-bell. "We have just finished in time for dinner," said Lady Thesiger. "Sir John will not be at home; he does not return until late."

I was tortured with impatience. Had I been waiting for a verdict over life or death, my agony would not have been one-half so great.

The long ordeal of dinner had to pass.

"You will allow me to go to the drawing-room with

you," I said to the mistress of the house. "I could not sit here alone."

Then I saw a chance. Agatha went to the piano and played one of Mendelssohn's "Songs Without Words." The difference between the pure, sweet, high-bred English girl and the brilliant, seductive French woman never appeared to me so great as when they were at the piano. Coralie's music wrapped one's soul, steeped one's senses, brought one nearer to earth; Agatha took one almost straight to heaven. Listening to her, pure and holy thoughts came, high and noble impulses.

Then, seeing that Lady Thesiger looked tired, I suggested that she should rest upon the sofa while I took Miss Thesiger for a little stroll through the gardens. The evening was beautiful, warm and clear, the golden sun lingering as though loath to leave the fair world to darkness.

At last, at last! My hands trembled with impatience as I drew the black lace mantilla over her white shoulders. At last, at last I had her all to myself, only the birds and flowers around us, only the blue sky overhead.

Then, when I would have given worlds for the power of speech, a strange, dull silence came over me.

"Agatha," I said at last, "I came over today on purpose to see you. I want to ask you something, a favor so great my lips can hardly frame the words."

She looked at me. There was infinite wonder, infinite gentleness in her eyes. I took courage then, and told my tale in burning words. I cannot remember now, but I told her how I had loved her from the first moment I had ever seen her, and had resolved upon winning her, if she was to be won.

Never mind what passed. I only know the sun never shone so brightly, the flowers were never one-half so fair, the world so bright, no man ever one-half so happy.

For she - well, she had listened to me, and her sweet lips quivered, her beautiful face had grown tender and soft; she laid her little, white hands in mine and said she loved me.

I have wondered since that the weight of my own happiness did not break my heart, the suspense had been so great.

"You love me? Say it again, Agatha. I cannot believe it. Oh, my darling, it seemed to me easier to reach the golden stars than to win you!"

"You did not try," she said, with a smile half sweet, half divine. "You always looked frightened at me."

"So I was, but I will grow bolder now. Such beauty, such purity, such goodness as yours would awe anyone. I can hardly believe now in my own good fortune. Say it again, darling."

She raised her sweet face to mine.

"I love you," she said, simply; and it seemed to me the words died away in the summer wind more sweetly than an echo from heaven would die.

"And you will be my wife? Agatha, promise me."

"I will be your wife," she said; and then, to my thinking, we went straight away to fairyland.

I do not remember the sun setting, although it must have set; for when my senses returned to me a servant was standing before us, saying that Lady Thesiger was afraid it was growing cold.

There lay the dew shining on the trees and flowers, yet we had not even seen it fall.

Charlotte M. Braeme

CHAPTER IX.

I would not leave the manor house until I had seen Sir John. Agatha did not go back to the drawing-room with me.

"What will mamma think?" she said, in utter dismay. "See how late it is; and the dew has fallen."

"I will tell her why I detained you, Agatha. You are sure that I shall not wake up tomorrow and find all this is a dream?"

"I do not think so," she replied; and then she would not stop for another word, and I went in to meet Lady Thesiger alone.

She was surprised when I told her. No matter what Coralie said about maneuvering, if ever I saw real, genuine surprise in any woman's face, it was in Lady Thesiger's this evening.

"You have asked Agatha to marry you!" she repeated, looking half bewildered; "and pray, Sir Edgar, what did the child say?"

"She promised to marry me," I replied, more boldly; "that is, of course, if Sir John and you, Lady Thesiger, have no objection."

"I am afraid that you have not taken that much into consideration. Asked the child to marry you! Why, Sir Edgar, how long have you been in love with her?"

"From the very first moment I ever saw her."

"Why," cried her ladyship, "Sir John told me you were in love, and had promised to confide in him."

Remembering what I had said to him, I explained to her that in speaking as I had done I referred entirely to Agatha.

"It is so utterly unexpected," she said, "that you must pardon my strange reception of your intelligence."

She sat quite silent for some minutes, then continued:

"It seems so strange for you to fall in love with Agatha. The dearest wish of Sir Barnard's heart was to have her for a daughter-in-law."

A fierce spasm of jealousy almost robbed me of my breath.

"Did she - did she -"

Then I could get no further.

"No, Agatha did not like Miles, if that is what you mean?"

"Did Miles love her?"

"I cannot tell - there was something very mysterious about him. He looked to me like one who had a secret

Charlotte M. Braeme

on his mind. I have often wondered what it could be. He was not a happy man of late years."

"You have not told me yet, Lady Thesiger, if I have your good wishes."

She held out her hand with a gracious, kindly smile.

"Shall I tell you the truth - no flattery, but just the simple truth? I would rather Agatha married you than any other man in the nation. She has not only my full consent, but I am pleased, proud and happy."

"And Sir John, shall I have his consent?"

"There is little doubt of it. I hear him now - he has just arrived, I suppose. You shall see him at once."

I rode away from Harden Manor that night a happy man. Sir John, like Lady Thesiger, gave his full, free, unhesitating consent. We had a long, confidential conversation. He told me how his affairs stood. He was a wealthy man, but his expenses were great. He told me frankly that he should not be able to give Agatha a large portion at her marriage, nor could he leave her anything considerable at his death. Harden Manor, with its rich revenues, was all entailed on his son.

"So that I am glad, Sir Edgar," he said, "she is likely to marry a rich man. She has been brought up in all luxury, and would never be able to bear privation. I shall feel satisfied of her future now."

Alas! so did I. I rode home through the sweet, gathering gloom and the starlight, one of the happiest men in England. I had won my love. She loved me whom I loved best.

There seemed to be nothing wanting then. Two short years ago I was poor, my daily life one of monotonous toil, without the least hope of relief. Now the silvery moon fell upon the woods and silvered the roof of the grand old mansion, and all this fair land over which I was riding was mine.

Coralie was waiting for me. She affected to be just crossing the hall, but I knew that she had been waiting there to have the first word with me. She looked eagerly into my face.

"How long you have been away, Sir Edgar! Surely the starlight agrees with you. I have coffee ready for you in the drawing-room - you have dined, I suppose?"

"Yes, I dined at Harden Manor. I have been there all day."

A dark cloud came for a moment over her radiant face.

"All day," she repeated. "Ah, poor Miles! If he rode over in the morning they were always sure to make him stay to the evening, if they could."

"If Miles found the place as pleasant as I do, the length of his visits would not surprise me," I said, laughingly. "I will run up to see Clare first and then try your coffee, Coralie."

I longed to tell my good news to my sister.

"Clare," I said, kneeling by her side, "look at me. Do you know, can you guess, what news I have to tell you?"

She raised her eyes to mine; she laid her dear hand on my brow.

"I can guess," she said, quietly. "You have told Agatha you love her, and have asked her to be your wife. Is that it?"

"Yes. She has promised, Clare. She loves me - she whom I have always looked up to as some queen so far above me."

"Any good woman would love you, Edgar," said my sister. She hesitated, then asked slowly: "Have you said anything to Coralie?"

"Certainly not. Why should I?"

A delicate color flushed my sister's face.

"To tell you the truth," she replied, "I have fancied of late that Coralie likes you. Nay, I need not mince matters; I am quite sure she loves you."

"She loves us both, because we are all in the world she has to love; but not in the way you mean, Clare."

But Clare shook her head doubtfully.

"I hope I may be mistaken; but, Edgar, I have a nervous feeling about it, difficult to describe and hard to bear, as though evil would come to you through her. I cannot tell you how the thought haunts and perplexes me."

I laughed, little dreaming then how it would be.

"Sheer nervous fancy, Clare. Take it at the very worst, that Coralie does like me, perhaps, a little too well, and is both piqued and angry at my engagement, in the name of common sense, I ask you, what possible harm can she do to me?"

"None that I can see; yet the dread lies heavy upon me, brother."

"You will forget it all, darling, when you hear the chimes of wedding bells. Ah, Clare, if you could get better I should not have a wish left ungratified."

Then, still smiling at Clare's nervous fancy, I went to the drawing-room. Coralie was there awaiting me. The picture, in all its details, rises before me as vividly as though I had only seen it yesterday.

Although the day had been warm, the evening was chilly, and a small fire burned brightly in the grate; the lamps were lighted, and gleamed like huge, soft, warm, pearls; the air of the room was heavy with sweet and subtle perfume. I have seen no woman who could arrange flowers like Coralie. The way in which she gathered them and placed each fragrant flower so that it could be most perfectly seen was wonderful. Great masses of crimson against white, amber and blue. She had the instinctive elegance of a true Parisienne.

It struck me as I entered that I had never seen so many lovely flowers; the vases and the stands were all full. Coralie herself sat in a large velvet fauteuil, the rich color of which formed a magnificent background to her bright face and golden-brown hair. She was

Charlotte M. Braeme

dressed with unusual elegance; a robe of soft, black crape fell in graceful folds around her. I never shall understand ladies' dresses, but this was made so that the beautiful, white neck and arms were bare.

I remember, too, that she had great sprays of heliotrope in the bodice of her dress and in her hair. She looked more lovely, more seductive, than any words of mine could describe, if I wrote for six months.

On the table by her side was a tray set with delicate china and silver, over which the firelight played cheerily. It was a picture of luxurious home comfort. She looked up as I entered with a grave, sweet smile.

"Your coffee is ready, Sir Edgar."

There was my favorite chair drawn up to the table. As I sat down I said aloud:

"This is comfortable."

Her smile brightened and deepened.

"You are like Miles, Sir Edgar. No matter where he went, he always said coming home was the most pleasant part of the day."

Then, with her white, jeweled hand, she poured out my coffee, and certainly the aromatic fragrance was very pleasant.

"You must be like Miles in something else," she said. "He always declared that I made better coffee than anyone else - better than he tasted in all his travels. Do you not think the same?" And she looked at me as anxiously as though the making of coffee to please me were the chief aim of life.

"Was Sir John at home?" she asked, after a few minutes.

Then I had to describe my day, to give her a history of the coming fair, in which she affected great interest.

"I should like to go very much," she said. "I have read in fashionable novels of fancy fairs, but I have never seen one. Are you going, Sir Edgar?"

"Lady Thesiger has asked my assistance, and I have promised it. We shall make up a party. If you wish to go, Coralie, you shall."

She thanked me, and when I had finished my coffee, rang the bell and ordered it to be cleared away.

"I am going to sing to you," she said. "I know you are tired. Throw your head back, shut your eyes and listen. Do not speak, because I am going to weave a charm for you."

I declare before Heaven that when I remember the magic of that charm my heart beats even now with fear!

Are you keenly sensitive to music, reader? If so, you will understand. I could neither sing nor play, but I loved music with a perfect passion. There was not a nerve or pulse in my body, not a thrill in my heart, that did not answer it. Listening to beautiful music, sweet, soothing and sad, this world fell from me. I was in an ideal life, with vague, glorious fancies floating round

Charlotte M. Braeme

me, beautiful, lofty dreams filling my whole soul.

In this higher world Coralie's music wrapped me; then I came to myself with a sudden start, for there was Coralie half kneeling by my side, covering my hand with kisses and tears.

CHAPTER X.

"Coralie!" I cried, in surprise. "What is the matter? What are you doing?"

She looked up at me, the fire of her eyes flashing through the mist of tears.

"Don't scold me, Edgar; it is the fault of the music. It sent me here to tell you how dearly I love you, and to ask from you one kind word."

I was terribly embarrassed. Could it be possible this beautiful woman was confessing her love for me?

"Do not judge me hastily," she said. "I am not like the fair, cold girls of this northern clime. My father had Spanish blood in his veins, and some of it flows in mine. My music went deep into my heart, and my heart cried aloud for one kind word from you."

"Am I not always kind, Coralie?"

"Ah, yes, with that cold, English kindness which kills even sooner than your keen frost and biting winds. I want something more than this cruel kindness. Oh, cousin, can you not see I love you? I love you - ah, heaven, how dearly! - and I want your love in return."

Charlotte M. Braeme

Believe me, reader, I was speechless. I would fain have raised her, have told her, in short, sharp words, that what she was saying branded her as unmaidenly and indiscreet; but I was powerless either to move or to speak.

"I loved you," she said, "the first moment I saw you. You are not like other men, Sir Edgar. You are so generous, so simply truthful, so noble. No wonder that I love you; no wonder that I look proud of my love. Ah, me! ah, me! would that I knew how to tell you! Give me your love; you shall never repent it. I will make home heaven for you. Men say that I have beauty and talent. Ah, me! I would use every gift I have for you; help you to win high honors that cold, unambitious natures never dream of. Ah, love me; love me, cousin! You will find no one else so true!"

Her face paled with passion; her glorious eyes, dim with tears, were raised to mine.

"Forgive me that I have spoken first. I should have died with my love. I know that other women in my place would have done so. I could not; life is strong within me. I could not die here, tortured to death by inches, without telling you. Ah, say to me that I shall not die!"

Weak words of mine cannot tell the passionate music of her voice, the passionate beauty of her face.

"You do not speak to me; you cannot forgive me that I have not borne my love and sorrow in silence until it killed me. Ah, see what love must mine be to make me to speak to you, to make me kneel to you, asking for my life, my life!" and as she uttered the words her head dropped on my arm, and her wealth of golden-brown hair fell over me.

God knows I would have given worlds to have rushed away. Never was man more unwillingly drawn into an embarrassing situation. And that very day Agatha had promised to be my wife. It was high time I said something. Gently as my patience and embarrassment would allow me, I raised the girl.

"Coralie," I said, gravely, "you are not yourself, I am sure."

"It is for my life," she said. "I am asking for my life!"

"You are easily excited and impulsive," I said; "that music has bewildered you. I do love you, Coralie; so does Clare. You are our kinswoman and our charge. How can we help loving you?"

"Ah, me!" she moaned, "you will not understand; it is not that love, Edgar. I want to pass my life by your side. I want your joys to be mine - your sorrows to be mine, darling; I want to share your interests. Will you not understand?"

"I do understand, Coralie. All the love of my heart is given - gone from me. Only this day I asked Miss Thesiger to be my wife, and she consented. All my love, my faith, my loyalty are hers."

I shall never forget how that fair woman rose and looked at me. The love-light and the mist of tears died from her eyes. All the lovely color faded from her face.

Charlotte M. Braeme

"You have slain me; you have given me, my death-blow!"

"Nay, Coralie; you are too sensible and brave."

She waved her hand with a gesture commanding silence.

"Do not seek to comfort me," she said. "You cannot. I have humiliated myself in vain. I have shown the depth of my heart, the very secrets of my soul, only that you may laugh at me with your fair-faced Agatha."

"Hush, Coralie; you have no right to say such things; what you have just said will never pass my lips. I shall not even think of it. You cannot suspect me of the meanness to talk to Miss Thesiger of anything of the kind."

She looked at me with a dazed face, as though she could barely grasp my meaning.

"Tell me it again," she said. "I cannot believe it."

"Listen, Coralie: I love Agatha Thesiger with all my heart, and hope very soon to make her my wife. I love her so dearly that I have no room in my heart for even a thought of any other woman."

Her face grew ghastly in its pallor.

"That is sufficient," she said; "now I understand."

"We will both forget what has been said tonight, Coralie; we will never think of it, but for the future be good cousins and good friends."

"No," she said, proudly; "there can be no friendship between us."

"You will think better of it; believe me, you have no truer friends than Clare and myself."

"If I ask for bread and you give me a stone, is that anything to make me grateful? But I declare to you, Sir Edgar Trevelyan, that you have slain me; you have slain the womanhood in me tonight by the most cruel blow!"

She looked so wild, so white, so despairing, I went up to her.

"Coralie," I said, "forget all this nonsense and be your own bright self again."

"My own bright self will never live again; a man's scorn has killed me."

Suddenly, before I knew what she was doing, she had flung herself in a fearful passion of tears in my arms. She was sobbing with her face close to mine and her hot hands clinging to me.

"With it all, Edgar, she does not love you; she loved Miles; she loves Crown Anstey, and not you. Forget her, dear; give her up. I love you. She is cold and formal and prudish; she is not capable of loving you as I do. She loves your fortune, not you, and I - oh, I would die if you bid me! Give her up, Edgar, and love me!"

When the passionate outburst of tears had had full vent, I unclasped her arms and placed her in a chair.

Charlotte M. Braeme

"Let us talk reasonably, Coralie. You ask me what is impossible. I shall never, with life, give up my engagement to Miss Thesiger."

A strange, bitter smile parted her white lips. I knew afterward what that meant.

"It is better to speak plainly," I continued, "in a case like this - better for both. Listen to me, and believe, Coralie, that even had I never seen Miss Thesiger, I - forgive me, but it is the truth - I should never have loved you with more than a cousin's love; my friendship, my esteem, my care, are all yours; more I can never give you."

Pray God I may never see another woman as I saw her then. She rose; with her white face and glittering eyes. Then came to mind that line:

"Hell hath no fury like a woman scorned."

"You throw the love I have offered you back in my face, Sir Edgar?"

"No, dear; I lay it kindly and gratefully in your hands, to make the joy and happiness of some good man's life."

"You distinctly tell me that you never did - never could love me?"

"I love you as my cousin, Coralie - not in any other way."

"You would never, never, under any circumstances, make me your wife?"

"Why do you pain me so, Coralie?"

"I want a plain answer - you would never marry me? Say 'yes' or 'no.'"

"No - since you force me into ungracious speech."

"Thank you," she said, bitterly; "I am answered - there can be no mistake. Sir Edgar, you speak your mind with honorable frankness. I have given you every chance to correct yourself, should you be mistaken. I am, perhaps, more richly endowed than you think for. Would my dowry make any difference?"

"No," I replied, sternly; "and, Coralie, pray pardon me; it is high time that this should end."

"It shall end at once," she replied. "It is to be war between us, Sir Edgar - war to the knife!"

"There is no need for war," I said, wearily. "Let us forget all about it. There will be no need for you to do anything romantic, Coralie. Stay on at Crown Anstey, and make yourself happy with Clare."

"Yes," she replied, with that strange smile, "I shall remain at Crown Anstey - I have no thought of going away."

She turned as though she would quit the room. I went up to her.

"Good night, Coralie. Shake hands, and let us part friends."

"When I touch your hand again, Sir Edgar, it will be

Charlotte M. Braeme

under very different circumstances. Good night."

She swept from the room with the dignity of an outraged queen, leaving me unhappy, bewildered and anxious.

I had the most chivalrous love and devotion for all womankind, and I must confess to feeling most dreadfully shocked. It seemed almost unheard of.

Then I tried to forget it - the passionate words, the pale, tearful beauty of that wonderful face. Strange that Clare's conviction should so soon be realized. What of that nervous conviction she had that evil would come of this fair woman's love? What if that were realized, too?

I sat late that night, dreaming not only of the pure, sweet girl I had won, but of the woman whose burning tears had fallen on my hands. What harm could she do if she tried? What did she mean by being richly dowered? Had she any fortune that I did not know of? Her words were mysterious. Strange to say, the same nervous forebodings that had seized Clare seized me.

Evil would come of it; how or why I could not imagine, but it would come. I felt it gathering round me; then I laughed at myself, at my own foolish fancy.

Yet the same fancy had shaken me so that when I went into Clare's room to say "Good night," she asked me if I were ill, and would not be satisfied until I laughingly told her my happiness had been too much for me.

I felt shy as a girl the next morning at the thought of coming downstairs to meet mademoiselle. Nor was I quite devoid of some little fear. Would she be sorrowful, resigned, pathetic, angry, or what? It was impossible to tell.

Imagine my surprise on opening the breakfast-room door to find her already at the table, looking blooming and beautiful as a June rose. She greeted me gayly, with bright smiles and bright words. I might have thought all the passion, the sorrow and despair of last night a dream.

Only too happy to imitate her, I began to talk of a score of indifferent matters. About everything she had some piquant, bright words to say. By the time breakfast was ended I had really begun to think I must have dreamed the most unpleasant scene.

Yet I thought to myself that I must be guarded. I must continue to be kind to her because she had no other friends, but all kindness shown to her must be of the true, cousinly type.

This morning, instead of lingering with her while she went through the conservatories, as had been my idle fashion, I went at once into Clare's room. Coralie noticed the change, for her face grew pale as I quitted the room.

Some weeks passed without anything happening. I went over to Harden Manor every day. The sun never set without my seeing Agatha, and every day I loved her more and more.

She was so simple, so tender, so true; now that she had promised to be my wife, there was no idle coquetry about her, no affection of shyness. She was simply

Charlotte M. Braeme

perfect, and it seemed to me that by some wonderful miracle I had reached the golden land at last.

Then I began to agitate for an early marriage. Why wait? Lady Thesiger told me laughingly that there was much to do at Crown Anstey before I could take my wife home.

"Remember," she said, "that before your sister came there had been no ladies at the Hall for some years. The late Lady Trevelyan died sixteen years ago."

I saw that she had completely forgotten the existence of mademoiselle, and did not care to remind her of it.

"You will want to refurnish a suite of rooms for Agatha," she continued; "and there will really be so much to do that if we say Christmas for the wedding, that will be quite soon enough."

"It seems like an eternity!" I said, discontentedly.

"It is the most picturesque season of the year for a wedding," said Lady Thesiger, "I like the holly and evergreens even better than summer flowers."

So it was settled; Clare agreed with Lady Thesiger that Crown Anstey required preparation for a bride.

"Those reception rooms want refurnishing," said my sister. "Of course, after your marriage you will give parties and balls. You will have to show hospitality to all the county, Edgar."

Half to my consternation, she said this before Coralie. I looked at her hastily, wondering how she would take it.

Her beautiful face was quite calm, and wore an expression of pleased interest.

"Do you agree with me, Coralie?" asked my unsuspecting sister.

"Certainly; there is no position in the county equal to that of Lady Trevelyan of Crown Anstey."

"How strange it is, Edgar, that you should be married, and your wife Lady Trevelyan! Sometimes it seems to me all a dream."

"Dreams come and go so lightly," said Coralie, with that smile which always made me slightly afraid.

The remainder of that day we spent in making out a long list of all things needful. Coralie's taste was paramount. She decided upon little matters of elegance we never even thought of. It was she who strongly advised me to send to London for Mr. Dickson, the well-known decorator.

"He will arrange a suite of rooms so perfectly that you will hardly know them," she said.

So it was decided. Mr. Dickson came, and when he found there was to be no limit either to time, expense, money, or anything else, he promised me something that should make Crown Anstey famous. All things went on perfectly. The magnificent preparations making for my darling occupied my time most happily. It was now almost the end of November, and our marriage was to take place on the 26th of December. Mr. Dickson and his army of workmen had taken their departure, and the rooms prepared for my wife were beyond all praise.

The boudoir was hung in blue and silver; it was a perfect little fairyland; nothing was wanting to make it a nest of luxury. The boudoir opened into a pretty little library, where all the books that I thought would please Agatha were arranged. There was a dressing-room, a bath-room and a sleeping-room, all en suite. Mr. Dickson had improvised a pretty flight of stairs leading into a small conservatory, and that opened into the garden.

When the pictures, the flowers, the statues, the rich hangings and the graceful ornaments were all arranged, I was more pleased than I had been for some time. Lady Thesiger came over to look at them, but my darling was not to see them until they were her own.

There was an unpleasant duty to perform. What was to be done with Coralie? Knowing Lady Thesiger's opinion of her, I felt sure she would never allow her daughter to live in the same house. What was to be done with her? Where was she to go? I did not know in the least what to suggest. I was perfectly willing to offer her a very handsome allowance, knowing that, as Sir Barnard's charge, she had some claim on me.

I might have spared myself all the trouble of thinking and deciding. One morning Mrs. Newsham, a pretty young matron, very popular in our neighborhood, paid us a visit.

Coralie, as usual, received her, and did the honors of the house. A very beautiful fountain had just been placed in the lawn, and we went to look at it. I had left the two ladies looking over the basin of the fountain while I raised the branches of a rare and valuable plant.

Stooping down, I did not hear the commencement of the conversation. When my attention was attracted, Mrs. Newsham was concluding a sentence with these words: "If ever you leave Crown Anstey."

I saw Coralie d'Aubergne look up at her with a quiet smile.

"I shall never leave Crown Anstey," she said, "under any possible circumstances."

Mrs. Newsham laughed.

"You may be married, or Lady Trevelyan may not like the place and wish it closed - a thousand things may happen to prevent you remaining here always."

But I saw Coralie d'Aubergne shake her head, while she replied, calmly:

"No, Mrs. Newsham, I shall never leave Crown Anstey."

I cannot tell how the words impressed me. I found myself repeating them over and over again - "I shall never leave Crown Anstey."

Yet she must have known that when my young wife came home, Crown Anstey would be no place for her.

Was there any meaning in the words she repeated so often, or did she say them merely with an idea of comforting herself?

Charlotte M. Braeme

It was that very evening that I sat by myself in the library arranging some papers, and thinking at the same time what I must say to Coralie, and how I must say it, when the door suddenly opened and she entered.

I looked at her, surprised, for she did not often intrude when I was alone and occupied. She was very pale. With quiet determination on her beautiful face, she walked up to me and leaned her arm on the back of my chair.

"So, cousin," she said, "this marriage is going on?"

"Certainly, Coralie. I pray to God nothing may prevent it."

"You would lose your reason, I suppose, if you lost Agatha?"

"I cannot tell. I only know that, no matter how long I lived, life would have no further charm for me."

She bent her head caressingly over me; her perfumed hair touched my face.

"Edgar," she whispered, "once more I lose sight of my woman's pride; once more I come to you and ask you - ah! do not turn from me - I ask you to give up Agatha, and" -

She paused, for very shame, I hope.

"Give up Agatha and marry you, you would say, Coralie?"

"Ah, dear, I love you so! You would never repent it. I

would make you happy as a crowned king."

I stopped her.

"Say no more, Coralie! I am grieved and shocked that you should renew the subject. I told you before I should never love any woman, save Agatha Thesiger, were I to live forever."

"Nothing will ever induce you to change your mind?" she asked, slowly.

"No, nothing in the wide world."

She paused for a few minutes, then she quietly lifted her arm from the chair.

"Has it ever struck you," she said, "it may be in my power to do you deadly mischief?"

"I never thought you capable of such a thing, nor do I believe that it is in your power."

"It is," she said; "you and your sister are both in my power. If you are a wise man, you will take my terms and save yourself while there is time. Of course, if I were Lady Trevelyan, my interests would be yours; then, if I knew anything against your welfare, I should keep the secret faithfully - ah! a thousand times more faithfully than if it concerned my own life."

She looked earnestly at me.

"You hold no secrets of mine, Coralie. I have no secrets. Thank God, my life is clear and open - a book any one may read. Supposing I had a secret, I should not purchase the keeping of it by any such compromise as you suggest. I detest all mysteries, Coralie - all underhand doings, all deceit. Speak out and tell me, Coralie, what you mean."

"I shall speak out when the time comes. Once more, Cousin Edgar, be reasonable; save yourself - save me."

She withdrew some steps from me, and looked at me with her whole soul in her eyes.

"I will not hear another word, Coralie. I do not wish to offend you, or to speak harshly to you; but this I do say - if ever you mention this, to me, hateful subject, I will never voluntarily address you again - never while I live."

She made no answer. She turned, with a dignified gesture, and quitted the room.

I never gave one serious thought to her threats, looking upon them as the angry words of an angry woman. They did not even remain upon my mind or disturb my rest.

CHAPTER XI.

On the following day Lady Thesiger had arranged to come to Crown Anstey with Agatha, for the purpose of choosing from some very choice engravings that had been sent to me from London. I asked Sir John to accompany them and stay at lunch. It was always a red-letter day to me when my darling came to my house, and I remember this one - ah, me! - so well. It was fine, clear and frosty; the sky was blue; the sun shone with that clear gold gleam it has in winter; the hoar frost sparkled on the leafless trees and hedges; the ground was hard and seemed to ring beneath one's feet.

"A bright, clear day," said Coralie, as we sat at breakfast together.

"Yes," I replied. "Coralie, will you see that a good luncheon is served today? Sir John and Lady Thesiger are coming - Miss Thesiger, too - and they will remain for lunch."

Her face cleared and brightened.

"Coming today, are they? I am very glad."

I looked upon this as an amiable wish to atone for the unpleasantness of last night, and answered her in the same good spirit.

Charlotte M. Braeme

I am half ashamed to confess that when Agatha was coming I seldom did anything but stand, watch in hand, somewhere near the entrance gates. That I did today, and was soon rewarded by seeing the Harden carriage.

Ah, me! will the memory of that day ever die with me? My darling came and seemed to me more beautiful than ever. Her sweet, frank eyes looked into mine; her pure, beautiful face had a delicate flush of delight, and I - God help me! - forgot everything while by her side.

We were all in the library. How I thanked God afterward that Clare had not felt well enough to have the engravings sent to her room, as I proposed! We sat round the large center-table on which the folios lay open, Sir John, who took great delight in such things, explaining to Lady Thesiger. I was showing Agatha those I liked best, when quite unexpectedly, Coralie entered the room.

The moment I saw her face I knew that she meant mischief. Surely, woman's face never had so hard, so wicked a look before.

Sir John rose and bowed. Lady Thesiger looked, as she always did in the presence of mademoiselle, const- rained and annoyed. Agatha's look was one of sheer surprise, for Coralie walked up to the table.

"Choosing engravings, Miss Thesiger?" she said, with an easy smile. "I must ask you to give me your attention for a short time. Perhaps you will not think the engravings of much importance after that."

She declined the chair Sir John placed for her with the

hauteur of a grand duchess. As she stood there, calmly surveying us, she looked the most beautiful yet the most determined of women.

"May I ask," she said, "the exact date fixed for the marriage?"

Sir John answered her:

"The 26th of December, mademoiselle."

"May I ask," she said, "what Sir Edgar has thought of doing for me? Doubtless Lady Thesiger will have advised him. This has been my home for many years, and is my only home now. Has the question been considered? In the event of Sir Edgar bringing a young wife here, what is to become of me?"

There was a mocking smile on her beautiful face; her dark eyes flashed from one to the other of us; we felt uncomfortable. She had just hit upon the weak point that disturbed us all, the one cloud in a clear sky.

As no one else seemed inclined to speak, I answered:

"Everything will be done for your comfort, Coralie; you may be sure of that, for Sir Barnard's sake."

"And not for my own?" she said. "What is your idea of comfort, Sir Edgar? Do you propose offering me a little cottage and a few pounds per week? That would not content me."

She looked so imperial, so beautiful, that I wondered involuntarily what would content her, she who might have anything.

Charlotte M. Braeme

"Whatever you yourself think right, Coralie, you shall have."

I saw a strong disapproval in Lady Thesiger's face, and Coralie's quick eyes, following mine, read the same.

"Ah!" she said, hastily, "Lady Thesiger does not approve of carte blanche to ambitious cousins."

Lady Thesiger really restrained herself; she was tempted to speak - I saw that - but refrained.

"The best plan," said Sir John, calmly, "would be for Mademoiselle d'Aubergne to say what she herself wishes."

"I will tell you," she replied, "what I claim."

Then, as we looked up at her in wonder, she continued, with bland calmness:

"I claim as my own and right, on the part of my infant son, the whole of the estate and revenues of Crown Anstey. I claim, as widow of the late Miles Trevelyan, Esq., my share of all due to me at his death."

A thunder-bolt falling in our midst would not have alarmed us as those words did. Sir John looked sternly at her.

"In the name of heaven, what do you mean?"

"Just what I say, Sir John. I was the wife, and am now the widow, of the late Miles Trevelyan, Esq."

"But that is monstrous!" he cried. "Miles was

never married."

"Miles was married to me, Sir John."

"But we must have proof; your word goes for nothing. There must be indisputable proof of such an assertion."

She smiled with quiet superiority.

"Knowing with whom I have to contend, it is not probable that I should assert anything false. I am prepared to prove everything I say."

My darling's face grew white as death. I was bewildered. If this were true - oh, my God! if it were true - fortune, love and everything else were lost.

"Where were you married?" asked Sir John.

"At Edgerton - St. Helen's, Edgerton. The Rev. Henry Morton married us, and the two witnesses were Sarah Smith, who was my maid, and Arthur Ireton, who was head game-keeper here at Crown Anstey."

It was so quickly told and so seemingly correct, we looked at each other in amaze.

"We must examine into it," said Sir John, "before going any further."

"That will be best," she replied, composedly. "I had better explain that Miles, poor fellow, fell in love with me the first time he saw me. Sir Barnard would not hear of such a thing. He told Miles that if he persisted in marrying me he would curse him. Perhaps he had his own reasons for not liking me. His son tried to

Charlotte M. Braeme

obey him, but I am proud to say that the love Miles had for me was far stronger than fear of his father. Still, for pecuniary reasons he did not care to offend him, so we were married privately the second year of my stay at Crown Anstey."

She turned to Lady Thesiger with a mocking smile.

"I know perfectly well," she said, "why your ladyship has never liked me. You met me walking one evening with Miles Trevelyan in the Anstey woods; you saw him kiss me. You know, now, that he was my husband and had a right to kiss me if he chose."

Lady Thesiger bowed very stiffly.

"Two years after our marriage," Coralie continued, "my little son, called Rupert, after the Crusader Trevelyan, was born. Under the pretense of visiting some of my relations, I went to Lincoln. In the registry of the church of St. Morton Friars you will find the proper attestation of my son's birth."

"Where is that son?" asked Sir John, incredulously.

"At Lincoln. I can send for him. You can go there and see him; he is under the care of Sarah Smith, my nurse. He is living and well, and he, not Mr. Edgar, is the heir of Crown Anstey."

"But why," asked Sir John, incredulously, "why have you never told this story before? It seems incredible that you should have waited until now."

"I have my own reasons," she replied. "I waited first to see what Sir Edgar would be like; then, when I saw him - I - I need not be ashamed to own it, even before Miss Thesiger - I liked him, and if he had been reasonable I should never have told my story at all."

"That is," said Sir John, with supreme disgust, "if Edgar had been duped by you and had married you, you would have defrauded your son of his rights?"

"Yes," she replied, with a smile; "it is Crown Anstey I love, and I would rather be the wife than the mother of the master of Crown Anstey."

"You are a wicked woman," he said, sternly.

"I am a successful one," she retorted. "Pray, Sir John, examine all these proofs at your earliest convenience; I am anxious to take my place as mistress of my own house; I am anxious to have my child here in his own home."

We all rose; no words can express my emotions. It was not the fortune, God knows - not the fortune; but I knew when I lost that I lost Agatha.

I felt my face growing white as death itself and my hands trembled.

"One moment," I said. "A year ago the doctor told me if my sister kept up her strength, and had nothing to make her either anxious nor unhappy, she would in all probability recover. Now, whether this story be true or false, I pray you all, for God's sake, keep it from her!"

"I shall not mention it," said Coralie.

"Do not despair, Edgar," said Sir John. "I do not

Charlotte M. Braeme

believe - I never shall!"

"I wrote to London last night," continued Coralie, "for Mr. Dempster, who was Sir Barnard's lawyer on one or two occasions. You, of course, Mr. Edgar Trevelyan, will retain the services of the family solicitors."

"I shall need no solicitors if your story be true. I shall not seek to defraud Miles' son of his birthright; I shall yield it to him."

"You will find it true in every particular," she said; "and remember always that it is your own fault I have told it."

With that parting shot she quitted the room.

"My poor boy," said Sir John, "this is a terrible blow to you."

"I am afraid," said Lady Thesiger, "that this abominable woman has spoken the truth. I always thought poor Miles had something on his mind - some secret. I told him so one day, and he did not deny it."

My darling came up to me with her sweet, pale face and outstretched hands.

"Never mind, Edgar," she said. "If you lose Crown Anstey I will try to love you all the more to make up for it."

What could I do but bless her and thank her? Yet I knew - God help me, I knew in losing my fortune I lost her!

CHAPTER XII.

The little party that had so gayly assembled in the old library broke up in the deepest gloom. Sir John was the only one who seemed at all incredulous.

"Rely upon it," he said, "that, after all, it is some trick of the French woman."

But Lady Thesiger had no such hope.

"I felt sure there was something wrong with Miles," she said. "He was not happy. He had married in haste and repented at leisure."

For my own part, I had no hope. Remembering the subtle, seductive beauty of the woman, I could well imagine Miles being led, even against himself, into a marriage or anything else.

When they were gone I went back to the library. I wanted to face this terrible blow alone, to realize the possibility that instead of being Sir Edgar Trevelyan, of Crown Anstey, wealthy, honored and powerful, I was Edgar Trevelyan, poor, homeless and penniless.

Could it be possible that after this life of ease, luxury and happiness, I was to fall back into the old position - hard, monotonous labor, with eighty pounds

Charlotte M. Braeme

per annum?

It seemed too hard. Do not think any the worse of me, reader, if I own that the tears came into my eyes. It was bitterly hard.

Without warning Coralie entered the room. It must have been a triumph to her to see the tears in my eyes. She stood at some little distance from me.

"Edgar," she asked, "do you hate me?"

"No! I am too just to hate you for claiming what is your own. You ought to have told me before, Coralie. It has been most cruel to let me live in this delusive dream. If you had told me that night when I came here first, it would have been a momentary disappointment, but I should have gone back to my work none the worse for it."

"I might have done it, but I saw in this, my secret power, the means of winning you. Edgar, it is not too late even now. Make me mistress of Crown Anstey, and I will find the means of restoring your lost position to you."

I turned from her in unutterable loathing. She was so lost to all womanly honor and delicacy, my whole soul revolted against her.

"Not another word, Coralie. I would not take Crown Anstey from you if the alternative were death!"

"That is very decisive," she replied, with the mocking smile I dreaded. "We shall see."

"You will keep your word to me?" I cried, hastily. "You will say nothing to Clare? She will soon be well. I could not bear to have any obstacles thrown in the way of her recovery. When I leave her, my friends will make some arrangements to spare her the shock of knowing why - at least, for a time."

"I shall respect your wishes, Edgar. I have no desire to hurt your sister. She is quite safe, so far as I am concerned."

It may be imagined that I did not sleep very well that night. Early on the following morning Sir John rode over.

"The sooner we look into this affair the better," he said. "We will ride over to Edgerton today and examine the church register."

We did so. Alas! there was no mistake; the marriage had been celebrated on the 14th of June. The two witnesses, as she said, were Sarah Smith and Arthur Ireton. The marriage service had been performed by the Reverend Henry Morton.

The entry was perfectly regular, no flaw in it. Sir John's face fell as he read it.

"Now," he said, "the marriage laws in England are very strict; there is no evading them. If this marriage is perfectly legal we shall find an entry of it in the registrar's books. We must pay for a copy of the certificate."

We went to the registrar's office. There, sure enough, was the entry, all perfectly legal and straightforward.

"Now," said Sir John, "before we rest let us find out the Reverend Henry Morton, and see what he knows about it."

That involved a journey to Leamington, where he was then residing. We found him without difficulty. He remembered the marriage, and had no hesitation in answering any questions about it. He knew Miles Trevelyan, and had remonstrated with him over the marriage. But what could he do? Miles was of full age, and told him frankly that if he refused to marry him someone else would.

"I have been ill and occupied," he said, "and have heard nothing of the Trevelyans since I left Edgerton. However, if my evidence and solemn assurance are of any service, you have them. They were properly and legally married; nothing in the world can upset that fact."

"So it seems," said Sir John, with a deep sigh, "Edgar, you have lost Crown Anstey."

The next day I wrote to Moreland & Paine, asking one or both to come over at once. Mr. Paine arrived the same evening, and looked very grave when he was in full possession of the case. He had a long interview with Mrs. Trevelyan, as we called her now; also with her solicitor, Mr. Dempster. Then he sought me.

"This is a bad business, Mr. Trevelyan," he said; and by his ceasing to use the title, I knew he had given up all hope of my cause. "Of course," he continued, "you can go to law if you like, but I tell you quite honestly you have no chance. The evidence is clear and without a flaw; nothing can shake it. If you have a lawsuit you will lose it, and probably have to pay all costs."

I told him that I had no such intention; that if the estate were not legally mine, I had no wish to claim it.

"It was a very sad thing for you, Mr. Trevelyan. I am heartily grieved for you."

"I must bear it like a man. I am not the first who has lost a fortune."

But Sir John would not hear of my final arrangements until we had been to Lincoln and had seen the child.

"No one knows the depth of those French women," he said. "It is possible there may be no child. Let us take her by surprise this very day, and ask her to accompany us to the house where the nurse lives."

Both lawyers applauded the idea.

"If there be any imposture we are sure to find it out," they said.

Without a minute's loss of time, Mrs. Trevelyan was asked to join us in the library. She complied at once.

"We want you to go with us to Lincoln to show us the child," said Sir John, abruptly.

She consented at once so readily that I felt certain that our quest was useless. We started in an hour's time, my poor Clare being led to believe that we had gone to Harden on a visit.

We reached Lincoln about six o'clock at night. While

we stood in the station waiting for a cab Mr. Paine turned suddenly to Coralie.

"What is the address?" he asked.

Again there was not a moment's hesitation.

"No. 6 Lime Cottages, Berkdale Road," she replied; and fast as a somewhat tired horse could take us we went there.

We reached the place at last; a row of pretty cottages that in summer must have been sheltered by the lime trees, and the door of No. 6 was quickly opened to us - opened by a woman with a pleasant face, who looked exceedingly astonished at seeing us. Coralie came forward.

"I had no time to write and warn you of this visit, Mrs. Smith. Be kind enough to answer any questions these gentlemen may wish to ask you."

We all made way for Mr. Paine. I shall never forget the group, the anxiety and suspense on each face.

"Have you a child here in your charge?" asked the lawyer.

But she looked at Coralie.

"Am I to answer, madam?"

"You are to answer any questions put to you; my story is known."

"Have you a child here in your charge?" he repeated.

"I have," she repeated.

"Who is it? Tell us in your own words, if you please."

"He is the son of the late Mr. Miles Trevelyan and his wife, who was Mademoiselle d'Aubergne."

"Where were they married?" he asked.

"They were married at the Church of St. Helen's, Edgerton. I was one witness; the other was Arthur Ireton, the head game-keeper."

"Where was this child born?" he asked again.

"Here, sir, at this house. Mrs. Trevelyan left home, it was believed, to visit some friends. She came here and took this house. I remained with her, and have had charge of little Master Rupert ever since."

He asked fifty other questions; they were answered with equal clearness and precision.

"Let us see the child," said Sir John, impatiently.

She went into the next room and brought out a lovely little boy. He was asleep, but at the sound of strange voices opened his eyes.

"Mamma!" he cried when he saw Coralie, and she took him in her arms.

Sir John looked earnestly at him.

"There is no mistake," he said; "we want no further evidence. I can tell by his face this is poor Miles' son."

He was a lovely, bright-eyed boy; he had Coralie's golden-brown hair, which fell in thick ringlets down his pretty neck.

"But it is Miles' face," Sir John repeated, and we did not doubt him. "There remains but one thing more to make the whole evidence complete. We must see the registration of the birth of the child, and it would be better to see the doctor who attended you, madam."

We did both on the following day. The registration of the child's birth was right, perfect and without a flaw.

The doctor, a highly respectable medical practitioner, offered us his evidence on oath.

There was nothing left, then, but to return to Crown Anstey and give up possession.

I loved the little boy. It was too absurd to feel any enmity against him. He was so bright and clever; it would have been unmanly not to have loved dead Miles' son.

Of Coralie Trevelyan I asked but one favor; that she would allow me one week in which to make some arrangement for Clare before she brought the young heir home. She cheerfully agreed to this.

"You bear your reverses very bravely," she said.

"Better than I bore prosperity," I replied, and that, God knows, was true.

This new trial had braced my nerves and made me stronger than I had ever been in my whole life before.

CHAPTER XIII.

The arrangement made for my sister was one I knew not how to be grateful enough for. Lady Thesiger insisted that she should go to Harden and remain there until she was well.

"She need know nothing of your misfortune yet. We have but to say that she must be kept quiet and admit no visitors except such as we can trust to say nothing to her. Agatha and myself will take the greatest care of her, and when she has recovered we will break the news to her."

I was deeply grateful. It was all arranged without exciting my sister's suspicions. She told her that for many reasons it had been considered better to put off the marriage for some time; that I was going abroad for a year, and that she was to spend the year with Lady Thesiger.

She looked wistfully at me.

"It's all very sudden, Edgar. Are you sure it is for the best?"

I steadied my voice and told her laughingly it was all for the best.

Charlotte M. Braeme

She asked where Coralie would be, and I told her that when she returned from the visit she was paying she would remain at Crown Anstey.

There was not a dry eye among the servants when my sister was carried from the home where she had been so happy. Of course, they all knew the story - it had spread like wild fire all over the neighborhood - yet every one understood how vitally important it was that it should be kept from her.

Can I ever tell in words how kindly Lady Thesiger received her? True friends, they took no note of altered fortunes. My sister was comfortably installed in the charming rooms they had prepared for her. Her favorite maid was to stay with her.

Then came the agony I had long known must come. I must give up Agatha. How could I, who had not one shilling in my pocket, marry the daughter of Sir John Thesiger, a girl, delicate and refined, who had been brought up in all imaginable luxury? Let me work hard as I might, I could hardly hope to make two hundred a year. In all honor and in all conscience I was bound to give her up.

I had no prospect before me save that of returning to my former position as clerk. Agatha Thesiger must never be a clerk's wife, she who could marry any peer in the land!

Talk of waiting and hoping! I had nothing to hope for. The savings of my whole life would not keep her, as she had been kept, for even one year.

I must give her up. Ah, my God! It was hard - so

bitterly hard! I told Sir John, and he looked wretched as myself.

"I see, I see. It is the only thing to be done. If I could give her a fortune you should not lose her; but I cannot, and she must not come to poverty."

Lady Thesiger wept bitterly over me.

"I foresaw it from the first," she said. "I knew it was not the loss of Crown Anstey, but the loss of Agatha, that would be your sorest trial."

Then I said "good-by" to her whom I had hoped so soon to call my wife. I kissed her white face and trembling hands for the last time.

But the dear soul clung to me, weeping.

"You may say you must leave me a thousand times, Edgar, but I shall never be left. I shall wait for you; and if it be never in your power to claim me, I shall marry no other man. I will be yours in death as in life."

And though I tried to shake her resolution, I knew that it would be so. I knew that no other man would ever call her wife.

The day before I left, Mrs. Trevelyan, with her little Sir Rupert, took possession of the Hall. She must have found many thorns in her path, for, although she had attained her heart's desire, and was now mistress of Crown Anstey, she was shunned and disliked by all the neighborhood.

"An adventuress," they called her, and as such refused

Charlotte M. Braeme

to receive her into their society. Perhaps she had foreseen this when she wished to marry me.

By Sir John's influence, the post of secretary was found for me with an English nobleman residing in Paris. I was to live in the house; my duties were sufficiently onerous, and I was to receive a salary of one hundred and fifty pounds per annum; so that, after all, I was better off than I had once expected to be.

I bade farewell to Agatha, to Clare, to my kind friends Sir John and Lady Thesiger. God knew the grief that filled my heart; I cannot describe it.

On my road to the station I met the Crown Anstey carriage. Mrs Trevelyan bowed to me from it. She was taking a drive with the little Sir Rupert.

"God bless the child!" I said, as his little face smiled from the carriage window. "God bless him and send him a happy life!"

It took me some little time to settle down to my new life. My employer, Lord Winter, lived in the Champs Elysees. He preferred Paris to England, because it was brighter and gayer. I often wondered how that mattered to him, for he lived only in his books.

I was required to assist him in making extracts, answering letters, searching for all kinds of odd information, and I do believe I learned more in that time than I should have done in a lifetime differently spent.

I became reconciled to it after a hard struggle. From Harden Manor I constantly received the kindest letters.

Agatha wrote to me, and although the word "love" seldom occurred in her letters, I knew her heart was, and always would be mine. She would never forget me, nor would that crown of all sorrows be mine - I should never have to give her up to a wealthier rival. Although she said nothing of the kind in her letters, I felt that it was true.

A year passed, and at last came good tidings of my sister; she was able to sit up, even to walk across the room, and the doctor said that in another month she would in all probability be able to take her place in the world again.

How that gladdened my heart! Lady Thesiger said she had not the least idea yet of the change in my fortunes, although she wondered incessantly why I was absent.

"Have no fear for your sister's future," wrote kind Lady Thesiger. "While Agatha lives at home she is a most charming companion for her. Should she ever leave home, she would be the same to me. We shall only be too happy if she will spend the rest of her life at Harden Manor."

I was grateful for that. Now, then, fate seemed kinder. I could fight through for myself, providing that my fragile, delicate Clare was safely taken care of.

Another six months passed. Clare knew all then and was resigned. God had been very good to her. She could walk; distance did not fatigue her, and the doctors thought it was very unlikely that the same disease would attack her again.

She wrote and told me about it.

Charlotte M. Braeme

"I was out yesterday," she said, "with Agatha, and we met the Crown Anstey carriage. Coralie was most gracious - overwhelmed me with congratulations, invited me to the Hall. And I saw little Sir Rupert. He is so bright and beautiful - the most princely boy I ever beheld. 'I am going to have a white pony,' he said to me, and I kissed him, Edgar, with all my heart. Coralie inquired very minutely after you, and asked me if I owed her any ill-will for what she had done. I said no, not in the least, and that I hoped little Sir Rupert would live to make her very happy. I am not quite sure, but I think there were tears glistening in her eyes when she drove away."

Some weeks afterward I received the following letter from Mrs. Trevelyan:

"My Dear Edgar - Once again, I address you - once again, setting pride and all things aside, I offer you Crown Anstey. You have been away some time now, and know how different is your present hard life from the happy, luxurious one you led here. Your engagement with Miss Thesiger is, of course, broken off. I hear she has a wealthy suitor - Lord Abberley. It will be a good match for her. Edgar, you will find no one in the world so true to you as myself. See, I forgot all the past. Once more I offer you my love, my hand, and with it, until my son is of age, Crown Anstey. I never intended you to give it up as you have done. I always wished to offer yourself and your sister an income sufficient for your maintenance. I have not done so before because I hoped that poverty would seem so hateful to you you would gradually come to think better of my offer. Is it so, Edgar? Will you recognize my love, my fidelity, my devotion at last? One word and all your troubles cease, you are back again in the beautiful old home, and I am happy. Only one word. From your ever loving, devoted

CORALIE."

I need not repeat my answer. It was, No! I was no more free, no more inclined to return to Crown Anstey than I had been to remain there.

After that there was a long silence. Agatha told me herself all about Lord Abberley; that he had been very kind to her, was very fond of her, but she had told him our story, and he had most generously forborne to press his suit.

Time was doing much for me; every hour was golden in its acquisition of blanks in my life were filled by books. God sent every one the same comfort I had.

CHAPTER XIV.

It was just three years since I had left Crown Anstey. Lord Winter told me I should have some weeks to myself, but he was so incessantly occupied I never liked to ask for them.

I had never seen or heard anything of Crown Anstey since I left it. At Harden Manor all was the same, unchanged and unaltered.

One morning, when I went into the library, a letter lay waiting for me. I saw that it was Coralie's handwriting, and my first impulse was to burn it unread. Why should she write to me again? Her letters only pained me. I threw it aside and began to work - in the busy occupation of the morning I forgot all about it.

I did not open it until evening. It was from Coralie, but it only held these few words:

> "Edgar - My boy - my beautiful boy - is dying. Come to me; for if I lose him I shall die, too. In my distress I would rather have you near me than any one else.
>
> CORALIE TREVELYAN."

Was it true, or was it an invention? Poor little Rupert

dying! Why, no one had even told me he was ill. Perhaps I had better go. No mother could be so cold and so wicked as to feign death for her only child.

Lord Winter raised no objections.

"It was not very convenient," he said, but of course he "must bow to necessity."

I was in time to catch the mail train. Eight o'clock found me the next morning in London, and, without waiting for rest or refreshment, I started at once for Crown Anstey.

It was only too true. I found my old home full of the wildest confusion; women were weeping and wringing their hands - the whole place was in disorder.

I was shown into the library, and in a few minutes Coralie came to me. I hardly recognized her; her face was white, her eyes were dim with long watching and bitter tears.

"I knew you would come," she said. "He is dying, Edgar; nothing in the world can save him. Come with me."

I followed her to the pretty chamber where little Sir Rupert lay. Yes, he was dying, poor child! He lay on the pretty, white bed; a grave-faced doctor was near; the nurse, Sarah Smith, sat by his side.

His mother went up to him.

"No better! No change!" she cried, wringing her hands. "Oh, my God! must I lose him? Must he die?"

He was my unconscious rival; his little life stood between me and all I valued most, yet I knelt and prayed God, as I had never prayed before, that He would spare him. I would have given Crown Anstey twice over for that life; but it was not to be.

"Do not disturb him with cries," said the doctor to his mother; "he has not long to live."

She knelt by his side in silence, her face colorless as that of a marble statue, the very picture of desolation, the very image of woe.

So for some minutes we sat; the little breath grew fainter and more feeble, the gray shadow deepened on the lovely face.

"Mamma!" he cried. "I see! I see!"

She bent over him, and at that moment he died.

I can never forget it - the wild, bitter anguish of that unhappy woman, how she wept, how she tore her hair, how she called her child back by every tender name a mother's love could invent.

It was better, the doctor said, that the first paroxysm of grief should have full vent. All attempts at comfort and consolation were unavailing. I raised her from the ground, and when she saw my face she cried:

"Oh, Edgar! Edgar! it is my just punishment!"

I did my best to console her. I told her that her little child would be better off in heaven than were he master of fifty Crown Ansteys. But I soon found that my words fell on deaf ears; she was unconscious.

"I do not like the look of Mrs. Trevelyan," said the doctor. "I should not be surprised to find that she has caught the fever herself. If so, in her present state of agitation, it will go hard with her."

He was right; before sunset Coralie lay in the fierce clutches of the fever, insensible to everything.

I do not like dwelling on this part of the story; it is so long, long since it all happened, but the memory of it stings like a sharp pain.

Clare came to nurse her, and everything that human science and skill could suggest was done to save her. It was all in vain.

We buried the little child on the Tuesday morning, when the sun was shining and the birds were singing in the trees, and on the Saturday they told us his mother could not live.

It was early on the dawn of the Sunday morning when they sent for me. She was dying, and wished to speak to me.

I went into her room. Clare knelt by her side. She turned her white face to me with a smile.

"Edgar," she said, "I am glad you have come. I want to - to die in your arms. Bend down to me," she whispered. "I want to speak to you. Will you forgive me? I can see now how wrong I was, how wicked to love you so much, and how wicked to tell you so. Will you forgive me, and now that I am dying say one kind word to me, and tell me you can respect me in death?"

I pillowed that dying head on my arm, and told her I should only remember of her what had been kind and good.

"You will only remember that I loved you, Edgar, not that I was unwomanly and wicked?"

"I will forget everything, except that you were my dear cousin and dear friend."

"You will marry Agatha," she said, faintly, "and bring her home here. I hope you will be happy; but, oh! Edgar - Edgar - when she is your wife, and you are so happy together, you will not forget me; you will stroll out sometimes when the dew is falling to look at my grave and say, 'Poor Coralie! how well she loved me - so well - so dearly!' You will do that, Edgar?"

My tears were falling warm and fast on her face.

"Are these your tears? Then you care a little for me. Ah, then, I am willing to die!"

And so, with her head pillowed on my arm, and a smile on her lips, she died.

We buried her by the side of Miles Trevelyan. After life's fitful fever she sleeps well.

From the first hour of her illness the doctor had no hope for her. I learned afterward that for some time before the child took the fever she had been ailing and ill.

It was such a strange life. Thinking over it afterward, it seemed to me more like romance than reality.

A year passed before the dream of my life was fulfilled and Agatha came to Crown Anstey. I need not to say how happy we were.

Lady Trevelyan is the most beloved and popular lady in the county; our children are growing up good and happy; we have not a care or trouble in the world, and the sharpest pain I have is the memory of Coralie.

Charlotte M. Braeme

Choose from Thousands of 1stWorldLibrary Classics By

Adolphus WilliamWard
Aesop
Agatha Christie
Alexander Aaronsohn
Alexander Kielland
Alexandre Dumas
Alfred Gatty
Alfred Ollivant
Alice Duer Miller
Alice Turner Curtis
Alice Dunbar
Ambrose Bierce
Amelia E. Barr
Andrew Lang
Andrew McFarland Davis
Anna Sewell
Annie Besant
Annie Hamilton Donnell
Annie Payson Call
Anton Chekhov
Arnold Bennett
Arthur Conan Doyle
Arthur Ransome
Atticus
B. M. Bower
Basil King
Bayard Taylor
Ben Macomber
Booth Tarkington
Bram Stoker
C. Collodi
C. E. Orr
C. M. Ingleby
Carolyn Wells
Catherine Parr Traill
Charles A. Eastman
Charles Dickens
Charles Dudley Warner
Charles Farrar Browne
Charles Ives
Charles Kingsley
Charles Lathrop Pack
Charles Whibley
Charles Willing Beale
Charlotte M. Braeme
Charlotte M.Yonge
Clair W. Hayes
Clarence Day Jr.
Clarence E. Mulford

Clemence Housman
Confucius
Cornelis DeWitt Wilcox
Cyril Burleigh
D. H. Lawrence
Daniel Defoe
David Garnett
Don Carlos Janes
Donald Keyhole
Dorothy Kilner
Dougan Clark
E. Nesbit
E.P.Roe
E. Phillips Oppenheim
Edgar Allan Poe
Edgar Rice Burroughs
Edith Wharton
Edward J. O'Biren
John Cournos
Edwin L. Arnold
Eleanor Atkins
Elizabeth Cleghorn
Gaskell
Elizabeth Von Arnim
Ellem Key
Emily Dickinson
Erasmus W. Jones
Ernie Howard Pie
Ethel Turner
Ethel Watts Mumford
Eugenie Foa
Eugene Wood
Evelyn Everett-Green
Everard Cotes
F. J. Cross
Federick Austin Ogg
Ferdinand Ossendowski
Francis Bacon
Francis Darwin
Frances Hodgson Burnett
Frank Gee Patchin
Frank Harris
Frank Jewett Mather
Frank L. Packard
Frederick Trevor Hill
Frederick Winslow Taylor
Friedrich Kerst
Friedrich Nietzsche
Fyodor Dostoyevsky

Gabrielle E. Jackson
Garrett P. Serviss
Gaston Leroux
George Ade
Geroge Bernard Shaw
George Ebers
George Eliot
George MacDonald
George Orwell
George Tucker
George W. Cable
George Wharton James
Gertrude Atherton
Grace E. King
Grant Allen
Guillermo A. Sherwell
Gulielma Zollinger
Gustav Flaubert
H. A. Cody
H. B. Irving
H. G. Wells
H. H. Munro
H. Irving Hancock
H. Rider Haggard
H. W. C. Davis
Hamilton Wright Mabie
Hans Christian Andersen
Harold Avery
Harold McGrath
Harriet Beecher Stowe
Harry Houidini
Helent Hunt Jackson
Helen Nicolay
Hendy David Thoreau
Henrik Ibsen
Henry Adams
Henry Ford
Henry Frost
Henry James
Henry Jones Ford
Henry Seton Merriman
Henry Wadsworth
Longfellow
Henry W Longfellow
Herbert A. Giles
Herbert N. Casson
Herman Hesse
Homer
Honore De Balzac

Horace Walpole
Horatio Alger, Jr.
Howard Pyle
Howard R. Garis
Hugh Lofting
Hugh Walpole
Humphry Ward
Ian Maclaren
Israel Abrahams
J.G.Austin
J. Henri Fabre
J. M. Barrie
J. Macdonald Oxley
J. S. Knowles
J. Storer Clouston
Jack London
Jacob Abbott
James Allen
James Lane Allen
James Andrews
James Baldwin
James DeMille
James Joyce
James Oliver Curwood
James Oppenheim
James Otis
Jane Austen
Jens Peter Jacobsen
Jerome K. Jerome
John Burroughs
John F. Kennedy
John Gay
John Glasworthy
John Habberton
John Joy Bell
John Milton
John Philip Sousa
Jonathan Swift
Joseph Carey
Joseph Conrad
Joseph Jacobs
Julian Hawthrone
Julies Vernes
Justin Huntly McCarthy
Kakuzo Okakura
Kenneth Grahame
Kate Langley Bosher
L. A. Abbot
L. T. Meade
L. Frank Baum
Laura Lee Hope

Laurence Housman
Leo Tolstoy
Leonid Andreyev
Lewis Carroll
Lilian Bell
Lloyd Osbourne
Louis Tracy
Louisa May Alcott
Lucy Fitch Perkins
Lucy Maud Montgomery
Lydia Miller Middleton
Lyndon Orr
M. H. Adams
Margaret E. Sangster
Margaret Vandercook
Maria Edgeworth
Maria Thompson Daviess
Mariano Azuela
Marion Polk Angellotti
Mark Overton
Mark Twain
Mary Austin
Mary Cole
Mary Rowlandson
Mary Wollstonecraft
Shelley
Max Beerbohm
Myra Kelly
Nathaniel Hawthrone
O. F. Walton
Oscar Wilde
Owen Johnson
P.G.Wodehouse
Paul and Mable Thorn
Paul G. Tomlinson
Paul Severing
Peter B. Kyne
Plato
R. Derby Holmes
R. L. Stevenson
Rabindranath Tagore
Rahul Alvares
Ralph Waldo Emmerson
Rene Descartes
Rex E. Beach
Richard Harding Davis
Richard Jefferies
Robert Barr
Robert Frost
Robert Gordon Anderson
Robert L. Drake

Robert Lansing
Robert Michael Ballantyne
Robert W. Chambers
Rosa Nouchette Carey
Ross Kay
Rudyard Kipling
Samuel B. Allison
Samuel Hopkins Adams
Sarah Bernhardt
Selma Lagerlof
Sherwood Anderson
Sigmund Freud
Standish O'Grady
Stanley Weyman
Stella Benson
Stephen Crane
Stewart Edward White
Stijn Streuvels
Swami Abhedananda
Swami Parmananda
T. S. Ackland
The Princess Der Ling
Thomas A. Janvier
Thomas A Kempis
Thomas Anderton
Thomas Bailey Aldrich
Thomas Bulfinch
Thomas De Quincey
Thomas H. Huxley
Thomas Hardy
Thomas More
Thornton W. Burgess
U. S. Grant
Valentine Williams
Victor Appleton
Virginia Woolf
Walter Scott
Washington Irving
Wilbur Lawton
Wilkie Collins
Willa Cather
Willard F. Baker
William Makepeace
Thackeray
William W. Walter
Winston Churchill
Yei Theodora Ozaki
Young E. Allison
Zane Grey